Hannah
from
Nonnie
2000

THE PRIVATE WAR OF
LILLIAN ADAMS

BOOKS BY
BARBARA CORCORAN

Barbara Corcoran

THE PRIVATE WAR OF LILLIAN ADAMS

A Jean Karl Book

ATHENEUM   1989   NEW YORK

The complete text of "The Soldier," by Rupert Brooke, may be found in *The New Oxford Book of English Verse, 1250–1950,* ed. Helen Gardner (Oxford: Oxford University Press, 1972).

Excerpt from "A Lament," by Wilfrid Wilson Gibson, published in *Collected Poems, 1905–25,* is used with the kind permission of Macmillan Publishers Ltd., London and Basingstoke, and with the special permission of Michael Gibson.

The complete text of "The Broomstick Train; Or, the Return of the Witches," by Oliver Wendell Holmes, may be found in *The Complete Poetical Works of Oliver Wendell Holmes,* ed. Horace Scudder (Boston: Houghton Mifflin Co., 1923).

Atheneum
Macmillan Publishing Company
866 Third Avenue, New York, NY 10022
Collier Macmillan Canada, Inc.
First Edition   Printed in the United States of America

10   9   8   7   6   5   4   3   2   1

Library of Congress Cataloging-in-Publication Data
Corcoran, Barbara.
The private war of Lillian Adams/Barbara Corcoran.   p.   cm.
"A Jean Karl book."
Summary: When her favorite cousin leaves for Europe to fight in the Great War, patriotic Lil looks for spies in her hometown of Brookline, Massachusetts.
ISBN 0–689–31443–4
1. World War, 1914–1918—United States—Juvenile fiction. [1. World War, 1914–1918—United States—Fiction. 2. Massachusetts—Fiction.] I. Title. PZ7.C814 Pt 1989 [Fic]—dc19 88–27485 CIP AC

*In memory of Ernest Tuck, my own
World War One hero*

THE PRIVATE WAR OF
LILLIAN ADAMS

Chapter ONE

0¦0¦0¦0¦0¦0¦0¦0

September 1917

LIL TRIED ON her toughest expression and stared at herself in the mirror. "Don't shove me," she growled in the new voice she had been practicing for this first day at a new school in a new town. "Just don't push me or you'll be sorry."

That didn't sound threatening enough. "Or I'll wallop you right in the geezer." That was better. She combed her bangs down over her forehead so she had to peer through her hair like Aunt Bett's sheep dog.

"Hurry up, Lil." It was her mother's voice calling up the stairs.

¦ 1 ¦

"Coming." Lil took her time buttoning up the long row of tiny buttons on her green-and-white-checked gingham dress. She pulled on her knee socks and found her black patent leather shoes under the bed. If she was slow enough, her mother wouldn't have time to tie the huge hair ribbon that she always insisted Lil should wear when she was dressed up. Lil remembered all too well the comments her stiff hair bow had caused when she went to that school in Boston.

"When is she going to fly?" they said. "Maybe she's a giant butterfly." And ruder remarks than those. Within five minutes someone had jerked the ribbon off the top of her head and hung it around her neck. Then the teacher scolded her for coming to class with a ribbon hanging around her neck. That was second grade, the year she had not spoken to anyone except when she was called on, the year she lived in terror of being beaten up on the way home. The teacher was Mr. Jenkins, and she had rejoiced when he resigned and joined the French army to fight the Germans. Later they said he had been wounded, and she supposed she was sorry about that, but it didn't excuse his being rude to her.

She had spent the third grade at home in the Brookline house getting over rheumatic fever. There were disadvantages to being sick all that time, like being in bed a lot and not getting to her friends' birthday parties or to the theater with her mother, but there was also the joy of not having to go to school, of having plenty of time to read and to play with the dollhouse her father had built, and listen to records on the new Victrola. Sometimes friends came over, and they played house and told each other horror stories.

But now she was facing another school, in a town twenty miles north of Boston. Pop. 1,749, the sign said. Her father had finished his residency at Boston City Hospital in June and established his own practice here. She didn't know anyone well yet except Jay Collier, and he was no good to her now because he was in the fifth grade, and she would only be in the fourth. During the summer they had played hopscotch and explored Cilley's Meadow and the woods near the Hunt Club, and they had waded in swampy Miles River. Lil's mother used to spend summers in this town when she was a girl, and she and Jay's mother were good friends. But none of that helped Lil now. Jay had made it clear he didn't want any fourth-grade girl hanging onto his coattails at school. She would just have to be tough and stand up for herself.

"Get a move on, Lillian." Her mother's voice was getting impatient. "You'll be late your very first day."

Lil took a last look at herself in the mirror, stuck out her jaw, clicked her back teeth like a rattler about to strike, and headed for the stairs. That teeth clicking was pretty good. She had never seen a rattlesnake, but she had read about them in her father's *National Geographic*. They sounded scary. Maybe she could hiss a little, too. A rattler didn't really have any teeth to click, she thought as she went down the stairs, resisting the urge to slide down the banister; it was the rattles that made that noise, but if you didn't have real rattles, you'd have to do what you could with teeth.

Her mother looked up as Lil came into the kitchen. Somehow her mother always managed to look pretty and well-groomed, even before breakfast. "Sit down, Lil. I'll bring your eggs. I can do your hair ribbon while you're eating." She glanced at Lil again as she stirred the eggs. "Why are you looking like Frankenstein?"

Lil smiled a small smile of satisfaction. If she was looking like Frankenstein, she was on the right track. But she could not look like Frankenstein with an enormous hair bow stuck on top of her head. "There isn't time for a ribbon."

"Lillian, why are you so difficult about hair ribbons?" Her mother made one of her dramatic gestures and spilled scrambled egg on the black iron stove. It bubbled and turned gray. "Oh, drat, look what you made me do." Before her marriage she had been an actress. Once she had a walk-on in a play starring Lillian Gish. But, as she often said, she had given up the stage for her husband and child, and she had named her daughter for Lillian Gish. Lil knew more about the Gish sisters and Peggy Wood and Al Jolson, from her mother's days in the theater, than she knew about Abraham Lincoln or even President Wilson.

Mary, the pretty eighteen-year-old girl who worked for them, came in, letting the back door slam, as she always did. Lil loved Mary, and she had tried to imitate Mary's Irish brogue until her mother protested in horror.

"Mornin' to youse," Mary called out in the voice that sounded to Lil like song. "It's the great day then, Lil. Are you ready?"

Lil made a face. Lucky Mary had only had to go through the fourth grade in the old country. If Lil could quit at the end of the fourth, she could possibly stand school that long. Then she'd be free to do interesting things, like join the Red Cross and save soldiers' lives in France. Lil longed to be a heroine. There was not much room for heroines in the fourth grade. She wished she were old enough to join the American Women's League of Self Defense and wear pants and a shirt and tie and one of those stiff punched-in hats like the soldiers'. Even the housewives drilled with real guns. Lil liked to go to the drilling field and watch the women do extended-order drill and rendezvous-on-the-double. She and Jay did some of those things, but it was not very satisfying with just two people.

"Eat hearty." Mary plunked Lil's plate of scrambled eggs and toast in front of her. "You'll be needin' your strength." She grinned at the look Lil gave her. Mary knew and sympathized with Lil's feelings about school. Her full white skirt swished as she went back to the kitchen, and a long bone hairpin fell out of her red-gold braids. Mary always seemed to Lil to be dancing.

Lil began shoveling food into her mouth as her mother approached, carrying yards of light green ribbon and a tortoiseshell comb. "No time," Lil said with her mouth full. "Got to hurry."

"Jay's mother said he'd walk you to school," her mother said, "but I don't see any sign of him."

Lil knew he wouldn't show up. He had made it very plain that he was not going to escort her to school. "Maybe he had to go early." Mrs. Collier and her mother were close friends, and Lil and Jay were kept busy avoiding their mothers' plans for them.

Lil piled marmalade onto the piece of rough-grained Victory bread and bit into it, making a face. One of her mother's ways of winning the war was conserving food. She had persuaded her husband to dig up a plot in the backyard for a vegetable garden, but it was Lil and Mary who did the weeding. Meatless Tuesday and porkless Thursday were carefully observed, and the Sunday drives that Lil used to look forward to had been cut out to observe gasless Sundays. In some ways the war was no fun at all. On the other hand Lil enjoyed the excitement, the boys in uniform, the women drilling.

Her father came into the room, fastening his cuff links and shouldering into his linen suit coat. He had been out nearly all night delivering a baby, and he looked tired. He was the only doctor in town, and indeed for several towns around.

He squeezed her shoulder as he went by her and took his place at the head of the table. "You look pretty."

She knew he was trying to cheer her up. He always knew when she was worried. "Did Mrs. Sanders get her baby?"

He nodded. "A bouncing boy. Nine pounds."

Lil tried to think how Mrs. Sanders would look without that big stomach. "Did it hurt?"

"A little."

Her mother, coming into the room with the coffee-pot, snorted. "It always hurts, don't you believe it doesn't."

Lil looked at her mother. "Did I hurt you?"

"Lillian," her father said.

"You bet your boots you did," her mother said.

Lil sat still for a minute, not chewing the toast in her mouth. It was hard to imagine herself a big bump inside her mother. In fact it was hard to imagine her mother's beautiful figure so distorted. "You must have hated having me."

"Lillian." Her father's tone was sharp. "Of course she didn't. Finish your milk. Do you want a ride to school? I have to look in on Mrs. Lawton up that way."

She shook her head. She would love a ride, but the moment would come when she had to get out of the new Buick touring car and go into school alone. It would be less conspicuous to walk.

"But I don't have time for a hair ribbon." She ducked as her mother approached her. "Tell her, Daddy."

He grinned, then took his gold watch out of his vest pocket and looked at it. "I don't believe she has time for a ribbon, Ella. She doesn't want to be late her first day."

"You always take her part." Her mother jabbed at Lil's head with the comb. "I don't know what you're thinking of, either of you. She looks like a little savage. She can't even see through those bangs."

The doctor looked appreciatively at his wife's long tan skirt and pale yellow shirtwaist with the jabot at the throat. "You're looking pretty chipper yourself this morning. Having coffee with Bess Collier?"

"It's the knitting circle." Lil's mother smiled, and Lil knew the change of subject had worked.

"May I please be excused?" She was already out of her chair.

"Come straight home at noon," her mother said. "Mary will have lunch ready." She glanced in the oval mirror over the buffet and gave her dark pompadour a pat. The front hair was folded back carefully over the "rat" that she bought at Mrs. Ellis's beauty parlor. "Evelyn's giving me a shampoo at one."

Lil's father winked at her, and she fled. In the kitchen Mary was talking to the woman who had replaced their iceman when he joined the navy. Lil watched her swing the heavy block of ice off her shoulders into the icebox, her tongs and the leather protector over her shoulders glistening with moisture. Lil was considering being an icelady, although Mary said that as soon as the war was over, the women would lose their jobs to the men again.

"Didja hear about Mr. Brandt?" the icelady was saying.

"Him that lives on Maple Street?" Mary looked as if she expected an interesting piece of news. She often said that the icelady was better than the morning paper. The icelady was also a great patriot, who considered it her duty to pass on rumors about any suspicious activities.

"That's him. With a name like Brandt, you gotta be careful."

"Why?" Lillian said.

"German. German as sauerkraut. Well, it was Johnny Taylor told me. Johnny said the boss called Brandt into the office and asked him a lot of questions, and when he come out, the boys called him Hun and made him crawl on the floor and kiss the flag."

"Oh, the poor soul," Mary said.

"Poor soul, my eye! Johnny himself heard the man say our sailor boys looked like little kiddies playin' games in them sailor suits."

Lil backed away a little, out of the icelady's line of fire. She herself had been reminded of little boys' sailor suits when she saw navy men. That didn't make her a traitor, did it? She'd have to be careful about thinking.

"A filthy foreigner is what he is." The icelady slapped the tongs over her shoulder.

Mary looked thoughtful. "I'm a foreigner meself."

The icelady laughed loudly. "Ah, Mary, you're a shamrock from the old country. You're all right."

When she had gone, Mary was still frowning. "I heard about a fellow in Boston that was arrested for criticizin' the YMCA. It don't seem safe to open your mouth."

"There's a war on," Lil said. She didn't like to see Mary look unhappy. "Anyway, they're nobody we know."

Mary gave her an odd look. "Somebody knows them."

Lillian didn't have time to figure out what that meant. She was collecting her pad of ruled paper, two pencils, and her Liberty Stamp book and putting them in her leather satchel.

"It's a cruel, wicked thing, war is," Mary said, "if you should be wantin' my opinion."

Lil was alarmed. "Mary, don't talk like that. Somebody might hear you."

"I thought this was the land o' the free." Then she looked at Lil's worried face and her own expression changed. "Off to school with you, darlin'. I'll fix you something special for lunch. Remember, don't sass the teachers."

Lil knew the neighbors were probably looking out the window to see the doctor's daughter setting off for school, so she skipped along looking happy and smiling. She wanted them to say to her mother, "Aren't you lucky to have such a good child."

But she soon slowed down. She had plenty of time, in spite of what she had told her mother. She had timed her walk to the schoolhouse at least a dozen times during the summer. She had examined the school from every angle, even scrambled up the drainpipe to look in the windows. It looked a lot like the hated Boston school, only much smaller. Big square rooms with maps, charts, blackboards, and a flag on a short pole. The battered desks had been carved by one pupil after another into a mass of initials and dates that looked almost like a foreign language. The chairs and desks were bolted to the floor with heavy iron stands. The blackboards were clean, but they wouldn't be for long.

She zigzagged from the grassy edge of the sidewalk to the field of wild asters on the right, and back again, making up rhymes. "To go to school, a kid's a fool. She should run far away, and stay." At times she had thought of running away. Once she had gone six blocks in Brookline, but she got hungry and had to go home. No one even knew she'd gone, so it wasn't really worthwhile.

A pony cart passed her, and the girl driving it lazily raised the handle of her whip in greeting. That was Janice, daughter of her father's patients the Wards, who were very rich and had a huge estate. Janice was seventeen, and Lil admired her. Not only was she very pretty and grown-up, but she had that pony. Lil would die for a pony, but her father said there was no place to keep one.

At the railroad crossing Lil stopped. The train to Boston was standing in the station, facing away from her. The gatetender was already raising the wooden gates, but Lil was cautious about railroad tracks. What if the engineer made a mistake and the train started backing up just when she was crossing the tracks? There she would be, flat as the bent nails Jay said he put on the tracks sometimes. People would say, "What a tragedy! That pleasant child . . ." And her mother would cry and cry, and forget that she had hurt when Lil was born.

She looked both ways. The train started up with a jerk as one last commuter, coattails flying, leaped onto the iron steps. The brakeman jumped on after him, and the train left with puffs of steam and a shower of cinders. She stepped carefully across the tracks, remembering Jay's story about the boy who got his rubber boot caught in the track and almost didn't get his foot loose before the train came. It might not be true, but she was not taking chances.

She picked up a stick and made a rat-a-tat-tat on the iron rails of Miss Emerson's fence. Then, in the square she crossed the street so she could smell the wonderful smells of the drugstore: the faint, cool mixture of vanilla and chocolate and unknown things. She longed to go in and buy some penny candy, but her mother had forbidden it.

The door was open, and she could see the marble soda fountain with its six stools, and Mr. Kelly with his hands on his hips. He waved to her. She knew him better than most people in town because her father got his pills and things there, and he often took her with him for a chocolate ice-cream soda. One of the best things about her father was his love for chocolate ice-cream sodas. When she rode around with him on his calls, they always ended up at the soda fountain.

She looked at the big Red Cross sign in the window: Our Boys Need Sox. Knit Your Bit. Maybe she ought to learn how to knit. Jay could knit. She leaned against the plate-glass window, thinking that if a person were a spy, he or she could knit socks out of material that would make the soldier's feet fall off. Or maybe some stuff that would explode when you stepped on it. The enemy was very smart about thinking up things to kill people.

A bicycle flew around the corner going fast. It was Jay. He rode right by her as if she didn't exist, which made her mad. He could at least have said hi. But there he went, riding no hands, the big show-off. She tried to think of the best way to get even.

Some girls straggled past her, talking a lot, with several boys behind them shoving and punching each other. Some of the girls looked at her curiously, and a couple of them said hi, but they didn't ask her to join them. She didn't care. She slowed down so they would get ahead of her. Other kids were coming out of the side streets, everyone heading toward school. They all knew each other, and Lil didn't know anybody except that stupid, no-good, miserable Jay Collier, and that kooky kid named Tootie Gallagher, who lived across the street from Jay.

At the paper store she paused to read the big poster in the window. It had Spies and Lies written across the top in big black letters. It began, "German agents are everywhere, eager to gather scraps of news about our men, our ships, our munitions." She had read it so many times, she almost knew it by heart. She especially liked the ending: "Show the Hun that we can beat him at his own game. You are in contact with the enemy *today*. Report the man who spreads pessimistic stories, divulges or seeks confidential military information, cries for peace or belittles our efforts to win the war. SEND THE NAMES OF SUCH PERSONS to the Department of Justice, Washington, D.C. Committee on Public Information, 8 Jackson Place, Washington, D.C."

Lil longed to catch a spy and send his name to the Department of Justice. That would make her a heroine, all right. Jay Collier would have to notice her then.

She edged toward the curb as she came to the shoemaker's shop. He was standing under the sign that stuck out over the sidewalk like a flag on a short pole. In faded letters it said Cobbler, Soles, Heels, Taps. Hanging from the end of the pole, creaking when the wind blew, was an enormous wooden boot, the high button-up kind that her grandmother used to wear. But this boot would have fitted a woman giant.

The sign said that the shoemaker's name was J. F. Panzi, but the kids called him "Fancy-Pantsy."

He was tall and stoop-shouldered, with thick black hair and a long, thick moustache. His small eyes peered at you as if he wanted to put you on his boot frame and drive nails into you. Jay said that on Halloween the kids pestered him till he chased them down the street yelling in some foreign language. She was looking forward to Halloween.

Lil tried not to look at him, but just as she passed, he dumped a bucket of water on the sidewalk. It was the only paved block in town, and maybe he just meant to clean it off, but she was sure he had meant to splash her.

"Hey!" she said. Drops of water rolled down her skirt.

He said something that she didn't understand, but she clearly understood the look of hatred he gave her. She backed away, and as he raised the bucket to throw out the rest of the water, she ran.

She was breathing hard as she came into the school yard. Her father was always telling her not to run because the rheumatic fever had left what he called "a slight murmur" in her heart. She didn't worry about it; "murmur" reminded her of the cozy sound the water made at night at the lake in New Hampshire where they went sometimes in the summer.

The first bell was ringing. She hung back at the girls' entrance. There were all sizes of girls crowding around the doors, from the new, scared-looking first graders to the high school seniors, who seemed to Lil already grown-up. Some of the older ones looked at her and smiled, and one girl said, "Are you the new doctor's girl?" She had a nice accent like Mary's, and Lil wanted to talk to her, but she couldn't get up her courage. She said yes so fiercely that the girl turned away.

They were moving, girls at one entrance, boys at the other. She was the last one on the broad stairs, which were worn into wide dents in the middle. The little girls went downstairs, and the bigger girls went up to the second floor. The high school students went to the top floor.

Lil found herself standing in the middle of the second floor, not knowing where to go. Some of the last of the children looked at her curiously. So she pretended to be rubbing out the wet spots in her skirt, although in fact they could no longer be seen. She ought to ask somebody where the fourth grade was. Maybe she should have stopped at the office downstairs. She knew the school had called her mother a couple of weeks ago to say they were still waiting for her grade sheet to come from the Boston school but not to worry about it. Jay's mother, who was there at the time, said, "Oh, those school people are always rushed to death. They don't have enough staff." Maybe they'd forgotten about her by now.

She watched a girl walking into the far room on the left, as if she knew exactly what she was doing. She was wearing a calf-length, faded blue skirt and a white shirtwaist with a rip in her collar. Lil felt too dressed up.

The second bell clanged like doom, and the last of the pupils raced into their rooms, pushing each other through the doorways.

The big hall, with its one drinking fountain and the large picture of George Washington, was looking more and more deserted. A girl with blond pigtails raced up the stairs, and Lil tried to stop her to ask where the fourth grade was, but the girl had dashed too quickly into one of the rooms.

There was a lot of noise and confusion. One of the teachers was yanking at a boy's arm and saying, "You, Casey, quiet down, unless you want to be kept an hour after on the very first day." Lillian hoped she wasn't the fourth-grade teacher. Maybe she would be expelled for being in the wrong place the very first day of school. She had to clench her fists to keep from running out of the building.

Chapter
TWO

0:0:0:0:0:0:0:0

SHE WENT TO the water fountain and pretended to be very thirsty. Maybe if she sneaked out, she could go for an all-day ride on the train, up to Portsmouth or somewhere. Or she could go to Boston and look for her cousin Ernie. They hadn't heard from him for a couple of months, and he was practically her best friend. He took her for rides on his motorcycle sometimes when her mother wasn't around. She used to sit on the handlebars, till she got too big. Now she sat behind and hung onto him. It was thrilling.

For a moment she forgot everything except riding

on the glossy black Harley-Davidson, hanging on for dear life, the wind blowing her hair. If she ever went to heaven, it would be on a motorcycle.

"Why are you hanging around out here?" It was a sharp voice right behind her. Lil jumped. The woman was wearing a black skirt to her ankles, a high-collared shirtwaist with long sleeves, and she had hair pulled back so tightly in a knot that it made Lil's head ache to look at her.

"The bell has rung." She frowned at Lil.

Lil swallowed. "I don't know what room I'm in."

"Then ask. Do you know what grade you're in?"

Lil almost said, "Of course I know what grade I'm in. I'm not dumb." But instead she managed to say, "Fourth."

"Well, you should have asked. You've got a tongue in your head—use it." Then, looking slightly less stern, she pointed to a room in the far corner. "Hurry up or you'll be marked tardy and have to come to the office. And see me."

For a second Lil thought there was a twinkle in the woman's eye, but that did not seem likely. She muttered "Thank you," and ran toward the room.

"Don't run in the hall." The woman's voice was loud enough to make children sitting near the door in the other rooms look up and smirk.

Children were milling around the fourth-grade room as the teacher assigned seats. Everyone looked up when Lil came in. The teacher, who was younger than Lil had expected, glanced at the clock, but she didn't say anything to Lil.

"Oscar," the teacher said, "you're third row by the window."

A sandy-haired boy with freckles slid into his seat and immediately grabbed the pigtail of the girl in front of him and stuck it into the inkwell built into his desk.

The girl yelped.

"Oscar! Martha!" The teacher looked tired already. "Fold your hands on your desks and be quiet. Bruce Landon, sit here, second row, second seat." She glanced at Lil, who hovered near the door, trying to look self-confident. "What's your name?"

Lil had planned to say "Lil Adams." Instead, she forgot and replied, "Lillian G. Adams." That was always a mistake. Sooner or later they'd want to know what the *G* stood for, and they'd ask if she was related to the Gish sisters or what? She'd been through that before. She wished her mother had named her for some actress nobody had ever heard of.

"I don't seem to have you on the chart, but take that fourth seat in the row by the door for now."

Lil started up the row. A boy in the third seat was

sitting sideways with his feet in the aisle. Lil waited for him to move, but since he didn't, she tried to step over him. He lifted one foot and tripped her.

She fell headlong, hitting her head on the iron base of the desk. Somebody laughed, and then there was silence.

"Oh, dear!" the teacher said. To Lil, her voice sounded far away.

The next thing Lil clearly remembered was leaning on the teacher's desk and saying, "It doesn't hurt."

The teacher started to lift Lil's bangs, then turned a little pale and gave it up. "You'd better go home and have your mother call the doctor."

Someone said, "Her father is the doctor," and they all giggled.

Lil's head didn't really hurt, but she would be glad to go home. "I feel kind of pale," she said. It occurred to her that it was the teacher who looked pale. Maybe this was her first day of school, too.

"Erwin," the teacher said to a large boy at the back of the room, "you take this little girl home. And come right back."

Erwin lumbered to his feet. "Yes'm," he said. He was broad and tall, with a sleepy, good-natured face. He sidled down the aisle, stepping over feet and books.

"Don't forget to come back, Hot Dog," a boy said.

"Silence." The teacher went back to her seating plan as Lil and Erwin left the room.

The floor of the hall seemed to tilt up toward her as Lil walked carefully to the stairs. She held onto the rail with both hands as she made her way down the steps. Once she got outside, the fresh air made her feel better, but she had the sensation of stepping high, like the horses in the Labor Day parade. She looked at her feet to see if they were doing the normal thing, but looking down made her dizzy.

Erwin was walking in a kind of shuffle about five paces behind her. When she slowed up, he slowed, too.

As they came near the shoemaker's, she angled across to the other side of the street. The man was standing in his doorway. When did he find time to fix shoes if he was always watching people? She shivered, then turned back to Erwin, and said, "Why don't you walk alongside of me?"

Obediently he moved up. "Hot, ain't it?" He mopped his broad forehead with a clean handkerchief. His worn corduroy knickers looked too warm for September.

"Yes, it is." She wanted to hang onto his arm so she wouldn't feel so unsteady, but she was afraid she'd startle him. "You're big for the fourth grade."

Proudly he said, "Been in it three years."

She felt confused. "Nobody stays in the fourth grade three years."

He looked as if she had praised him. "I did. Two years in the first grade."

She didn't know what to say. Erwin would be an old man by the time he got out of grammar school. He seemed nice. They ought not to do that to him. "Is your name Erwin? Erwin what?"

"Erwin P. Anderson. Ever'body calls me Hot Dog."

"Why?"

He wrinkled his forehead. "I can't remember."

She felt sorry for him, but her head had begun to throb and it was hard to think of what more to say. "My cousin Ernie's got a motorcycle," she told him finally.

Hot Dog perked up. "What kind?"

"Harley-Davidson."

"She go fast?"

"Like the wind. I rode on it."

Hot Dog considered what she had said. "I'd like me a ride on one of them."

"Next time Ernie comes, I'll ask him."

He gave her a look of pure devotion. "I'd be obliged."

When they reached her house, Hot Dog stopped at the beginning of the front walk.

She said, "You want a glass of milk or anything?"

He shook his head and waited while she went up the walk.

"Thanks for bringing me home."

He just stood there, waiting. She opened the door and went in. Her mother was hanging up the telephone, and she was crying. Mary stood beside her, trying to comfort her. Lil thought the school must have telephoned, and she felt touched that her mother cared so much that she had banged her head.

"I'm all right, Mama," she said.

They turned to look at her.

Her mother said, "Ernie's enlisted. Two months ago! Oh, Lord, he'll get himself killed!"

"Now, now, now," Mary murmured.

They hadn't been thinking about Lil at all.

Then her mother reacted. "Why aren't you in school?"

Mary came toward her. Her face seemed to Lil to grow bigger and then smaller and bigger again, swaying toward her like a ghost. "What's the matter, Lil?" she said. "What is it, lovey?"

Her mother came up to her and said, "Oh, heaven preserve us, her bangs are bleeding!"

Then she was lying on her back on the operating table in her father's office, Mary holding her hand. Her mother was phoning one place after another, with the list in her hand that her father always left telling where he would be. Lil felt sleepy.

"Don't let her go to sleep," her mother kept saying. "Don't let her go to sleep, Mary."

"And why not, for the love of God?" Mary sounded upset, which was not like her.

"They shouldn't go to sleep after a concussion. Or

a skull fracture or whatever it is. . . . Mrs. Jackson? Is the doctor there? This is Mrs. Adams . . . We have an emergency. . . ."

"'Tis only a clap on the head," Mary said.

"Oh, Harry, it's Lil. She's cut her head open. Right on the temple. . . . All right, but hurry. And Harry, Ernie has enlisted, and I know he'll be killed. . . ." Lil's mother started to cry. "My favorite nephew, only seventeen and almost an orphan. . . ." Her tone changed. "All right, but hurry." She hung up. "He'll be here in a few minutes. He said she could go to sleep." She wiped her eyes. "He says the war will be over before Ernie gets out of training."

"I told you so," Mary said.

They seemed far away. Lil thought about Ernie riding his motorcycle straight at the Germans. He wouldn't get killed. Ernie was too smart, and the Harley-Davidson went like the wind. . . .

Her mother's voice curled over her like smoke. ". . . if she'd been wearing that lovely new ribbon, it would have been ruined."

And Mary's voice like soft music: "Ruined entirely."

Chapter
THREE

0:0:0:0:0:0:0:0

IN THE MIDDLE of the afternoon Lil awoke from a nap to see Jay sitting stiffly beside the bed with a small geranium plant held on his knees. Mary was hovering in the background.

"I'll bring some tea," she said, and left the room.

"I don't like tea." Jay's freckled face was frowning.

"What's that thing you're holding?" Lil said. She knew he must have come right after school because he was still wearing his good short pants and a clean shirt. His knees, tanned and covered with scars and scabs, looked bony.

"My mother sent it." He looked down at the clay pot as if he were surprised to find it in his hands. "Because you cracked your head open."

Lil gently touched the gauze patch on her temple. That was how wounded doughboys looked in pictures, only usually their bandages were bloody. "Is my bandage bloody?"

"Nah. But you look like you might have been in a battle. A small one." Jay's father was a training officer at Fort Devens. Jay wore his father's old garrison cap on his head most of the time, even to bed. Lil would have died for a cap like that, a real one that had belonged to a real soldier.

"Hot Dog Somebody brought me home."

"Yeah. He said you was pretty bloody." Last summer Jay had broken his wrist and worn a cast for weeks, to Lillian's immense envy. Now he could envy her for a while. Maybe you could be a heroine in the fourth grade after all.

"But don't go expecting any medal," Jay said. "Falling down isn't what you'd call patriotism. What were you doing in the fourth grade anyway?"

"It's my grade."

"Nah, it isn't." He sounded disgusted. "They placed you in the fifth, but the office forgot to phone your mother back."

She sat up straight. "I don't have to do the fourth at all?"

"Nope."

"I'm in the same grade as you?" She couldn't believe it.

"Just because you got tutored so good when you were home with whatever you had."

Mary came into the room with two cups of milky tea.

"No, thank you," Jay said, before it had even been offered.

"No? Well, your loss then. In Ireland all the big fellas drink tea. That's how they get so big."

Jay looked at her suspiciously. She handed him the cup and he took a sip, trying not to make a face.

"Mary, I got promoted! I'm in the fifth grade!"

"Good. That's one year out of the way. How's your headache?"

"I think it's gone. Hey, maybe I could skip every other grade and get clear through high school and all in four years."

"I'll tell you somethin' nice if you'll promise not to yell and jump around and start bleedin'."

"What is it?"

"Promise? Your ma will scalp me if you get all worked up."

"I'm not *worked up*!"

"Well, now." Mary grinned at Lil's impatience. "Somebody's coming to pay you a visit. Just a wee short visit, mind you, but . . ."

"Who? Who's coming?"

"Your crazy cousin, him with the motorcycle, him that's daft enough to go and join the navy. . . ."

"Ernie!"

"I told him and told him it was folly. Wait till they say 'Uncle Sam wants YOU,' I told him. That's soon enough surely. . . ."

Lil interrupted her. "Is he really coming?"

"Navy," Jay said in disgust. "He'll never get any battles in the navy."

"Please, God," Mary said and crossed herself. "He'll be here this afternoon, and don't you be gettin' up, Lil, or your mother will skin me alive."

Lil sat back, but she was smiling all over her face. She pulled impatiently at the high collar of her nightgown. "I have to get up, Mary."

"Is he coming on his motorcycle?" Jay asked.

"I daresay he'll come on the train, all proper and navified," Mary said.

"No, he'll be here on the motorcycle," Lil's mother said as she appeared in the doorway. "He's going to leave it in our barn. And you are supposed to be resting. I told you, Mary . . ."

"Can I keep the child down?" Mary said indignantly.

"The saints themselves couldn't hold her, in my opinion." She flounced her skirt and went out of the room.

"That Mary," her mother said. "She'll be the death of me."

"I'm resting," Lil said. "I feel calm as anything." It always worried her when her mother and Mary argued. She was afraid Mary would take it into her head to leave.

Her mother put the palm of her hand on Lil's head. "Wasn't it nice and thoughtful of Jay to bring you that pretty plant?" She smiled at Jay, who squirmed uncomfortably. "I hope you thanked him for his thoughtfulness."

Lil shot a glance at Jay's frowning face. "Thank you, Jay," she said demurely, "for your thoughtful plant." As her mother left the room, Lil said softly, "Geraniums make me sneeze."

Jay took another sip of tea, made a face, and put the cup on the bedside table. He stood up, his duty done. "So long."

"See you in the fifth grade," Lil called after him. She settled herself comfortably. It had turned out to be a good day after all, in spite of school and Fancy Pantsy. Her head ached only a little, Jay had brought her a silly little plant, and Ernie was coming. Maybe by tomorrow America would have won the war, and Ernie would marry Mary and stay here forever.

Chapter
FOUR

◻︎◻︎◻︎◻︎◻︎◻︎◻︎◻︎◻︎

SHE BEGAN AT ONCE to listen for Ernie. She heard Mary going around with the carpet sweeper, singing Irish songs, and her mother somewhere in the house, singing Victor Herbert off-key. She heard the ring of the doorbell and the muffled voices of her father's patients. Not many came to the office, not having any way to get there except to walk. There were only five or six automobiles in town, and not many people kept carriage horses. So her father stayed at home only one afternoon a week.

The screen door slammed shut, and a patient's tottery

footsteps sounded unevenly on the front steps. Lil stretched out her long legs. She had been trying to read *Treasure Island*, but even the exploits of Black Dog could not keep her from listening for Ernie's motorcycle. It was like all those months when she was well enough to sit up but not well enough to be allowed out, and she had waited and waited for something to happen.

Suddenly she heard the throb and sputter of the motorcycle. She leaped to her feet, clutching her bathrobe around her, and raced for the stairs.

"Lillian!" Her mother was already at the door. "You're not supposed to be running around." But Lil knew her mother was too pleased about seeing Ernie to scold her. Her father came out of the office, smelling faintly of iodine and ether and the other office smells that Lil was used to. He was grinning broadly. But Mary beat them all to the front steps, and she was the first to throw her arms around Ernie.

It was a different Ernie, more grown-up-looking in his tight, wide-bottomed, navy blue pants, his middy blouse, and the white cap that looked glued to his head at a rakish angle.

"They cut your hair," Lil said when she got her turn to hug him. "You look funny." His straight blond hair had been cut almost to his scalp. His head looked like a brush.

He swung her around, laughing. "What do you mean, look funny? I look swell! I'm the U.S. Navy, kid. I'm going to lick those Huns all by myself." He kissed the top of her head. "I will give you my medals."

"Oh no, you won't," Mary said, hugging him again. "I got first dibs."

"Fight over me, girls." He reached out and squeezed Lil's dad's arm. "How's my favorite uncle-in-law? Cured everybody in town yet?"

"Just about." Lil's father was laughing. Ernie made everybody laugh and feel good. You never knew when he'd show up or what he'd been up to, but all of a sudden there he'd be, looking great and making you laugh.

"Come play the piano." Lil tripped over Ernie's tall white ditty bag as she tried to pry him loose from Mary. She and Ernie had a great time playing duets together.

"Lillian," her mother said, "you're supposed to be in bed."

"What?" Ernie looked concerned. "You aren't sick again, are you?"

"No, I fell down at school and cracked my head." She lifted her bangs and showed him the patch.

"Walking wounded." He looked at her father. "No real damage? Brains didn't fall out or anything?" He was being funny, but Lil knew he was serious about wanting to be sure she was all right.

"You know Lil," her father said. "A tough nut, that one." He squeezed her shoulder. "Just as well to take it easy for a few days though, punkin."

"Tell you what," Ernie said to her, "you park yourself on the sofa, and I'll play you a new song before supper." He looked at his aunt. "I hope I'm not too late for chow."

"Oh, the saints!" Mary whirled away. "You're makin' me forget the roast. It'll be purely charcoal." She ran for the kitchen.

In the living room Ernie played "Anchors Aweigh" with one finger. "Remember it now, and when I come home on leave, we'll work up a duet."

"We could do it after supper."

"Nope. I got a date with you know who."

Lil knew who all right. He was sweet on Mary, and she on him. "You going to get married before you go?" She was very much in favor of their getting married. They were her two favorite people.

He looked almost sad for a moment. "When I come home, maybe." He played "I Love Coffee, I Love Tea," singing his own words in his soft tenor: "I love the ocean, I love the sea, I love the navy, and the navy loves me." She joined him for a second chorus. She wanted to laugh, but there was something about Ernie sitting there in his uniform, saying "when I come home," that made her want to cry. What if the Huns got him? Quickly she put the thought out of her mind. Nobody could get Ernie. "We're having steamed chocolate pudding with whipped cream."

He laughed. "Beats navy chow."

"I wish I had a hat like that."

"Wait till you see the other one." He ran into the hall and rummaged in the kit bag. He came up with one of the flat-topped, dark blue navy hats that Lil had admired on other sailors. It was round like a pancake, the material stretched tight over a hoop, and "USN" was sewn on the leather band in front. He clapped it on his head. "How do ya like that?"

She inspected him. "Good, but I like the white one better." She couldn't imagine why, but she felt like crying as Ernie stood there in his uniform.

"Supper on the table!" Mary's voice lilted from the doorway. Ernie sailed his hat across the room and dashed for the dining room, putting his arm around Mary as he went.

It seemed to Lil that people in love did an awful lot of hugging. But you had to put up with it. Supper was good: rare roast beef and Mary's scalloped potatoes and the horseradish sauce that Ernie loved. Ernie talked and talked. He answered a lot of her father's questions about the process of turning boys into sailors, but some of the questions he couldn't answer. "Military secrets," he'd say, looking solemn. And her father would nod and ask about something else.

Mary was looking at Ernie as if he had turned into some kind of hero already, and Lil knew just how she felt. He seemed older, old enough to be in charge of important things. It made Lil feel goose-pimply with pride, but it also scared her.

She knew by the look of them that Ernie and Mary were holding hands under the table. Ernie was trying to eat with his left hand and making a mess of it. Mary was giggling.

"Old Fancy Pantsy threw water on me this morning," Lil said, wanting some attention. She reached for a baking-powder biscuit.

"Oh, Lillian, he didn't," her mother said. "And *ask* when you want something; don't reach. And don't make up stories."

"He did, though. Honest. Is Fancy Pantsy a German?" Lil asked. "Maybe he's a spy or something."

"Lillian!" Her father's voice was sharp. "Stop calling the man by that absurd name. And no, he is not a German or any kind of spy. You could get a person in serious trouble, going around saying things like that."

"I'm sorry," Lil said meekly. But it would sure stir

up a storm, she thought gleefully. If she could find a spy somewhere around here, this town would sit up and take notice of her, all right all right.

"Mr. Panzi is an old man," her father said. "He's had a lot of trouble. Give him some respect."

"Oh, he's just a crazy foreigner," Ernie said. "He don't mean any harm."

"Foreigners are not necessarily crazy," Lil's father said.

Ernie made a rueful face. "Always putting my foot in it."

Looking at Ernie with his strange short haircut and his clear blue eyes, Lil wished with all her heart that she could do something to be worthy of him. She'd do what the government posters said, listen carefully to what people said, especially strangers. She might spot a traitor somewhere, and that would help the war effort and bring Ernie home faster. She squeezed her eyes tight shut for a moment and prayed, "Please, God, let me help get Ernie through the war in good shape."

"Eat your salad, Lillian," her mother said. "And, Ernest, Mary can't eat her supper if you clutch her hand under the table. She's not going to fly away."

"But *he* is," Mary said softly.

"The war will be over before he gets out of training."

Ernie looked serious. "I'm out now. I've been at the

Charlestown Navy Yard for two months, Auntie. Training goes mighty fast these days."

"And you told us you were going to vocational school!"

He grinned. "I was. In a way."

Lil's mother looked upset. She patted the top of her pompadour. Lil always knew she was nervous when she did that. Ernie was her dead sister's only child.

"I suppose they'll ship you right out," Lil's father said, and then noticing the expression on his wife's face, he looked as if he wanted to take back the words.

"Oh, sure," Ernie said.

"I wonder what kind of a ship."

"Can't talk about it," Ernie said. "Top secret." He stuck out his chin in the way he did when he was feeling pleased with himself.

"You won't get hurt, will you, Ernie?" Lil said.

"You know me, kid. I live a charmed life."

"Amen," her mother said softly, and Mary crossed herself.

"Don't be tempting fate." She piled more potatoes on his plate as if to protect him from the Germans with an armor of starch.

"You'll learn to pick up after yourself, anyway," Lil's mother said, "and that will be a blessing."

"I'm neat as a pin already. Shipshape." Ernie leaned back and patted his lean stomach. "I'm full, folks."

Lil felt deserted when, after the dishes were done, Mary and Ernie left, and she had to go to bed. She heard the motorcycle roar off and imagined the two of them riding into the soft night wind, laughing and loving each other. They'd probably head for Singing Beach and walk on the squeaky sand and chase each other right up to the edge of the water. Then they'd sit down and hug. People in love were strange, but she envied them a little just the same.

She tried to think about something else. Thinking too much about Ernie made her mind slide over to dangerous things, to a vision of something terrible happening to him. Ernie was her dearest friend in all the world. She listened to the rustle of the elm's leaves outside her window and the voices of boys riding their bicycles past the house. She thought about Fancy Pantsy. Foreigners were the enemy. But Mary was a foreigner, and there was nothing scary about Mary. Maybe there were different kinds of foreigners. The French, for instance; they were on our side. She'd have to make a list of the ones who were good ones and the ones who were suspicious characters. Her father said Fancy Pantsy wasn't a German, but what was he then? She thought of getting up and looking at the big revolving globe that stood in the corner of her room, but she was too sleepy to get out of bed.

She touched the bandage on her head and resisted the urge to pull the tape off. It itched. A lot had happened today, that was for sure. She had gone to a new school, landed in the wrong room, cracked her head open, been promoted, seen Ernie in his sailor suit, and had water thrown at her by Fancy Pantsy. She'd have to be careful not to call him that in front of her father. All the kids did, though. She wondered if Jay had thought about Fancy Pantsy maybe being a spy. If he hadn't, that would make his eyes pop open!

She yawned. The one other thing that had come up today, the thing she didn't want to think about, was that Ernie's training was over, and he wouldn't just be walking around in a cute sailor suit.

When she woke in the morning, a white navy cap lay on her pillow. Beside it was a note in Ernie's scrawl: "Dream about butterflies. Love, Ernie."

He was gone to the war.

Chapter
FIVE

WHEN LIL TOOK her absence excuse into the office several days later, the woman who had directed her to the fourth grade on the first day of school was the one who took it. She read it.

"Didn't stay long in the fourth grade, did you?" This time she definitely smiled as she stamped the letter and made out a pass for the fifth-grade teacher.

"It was a mistake," Lil said. "Nobody told me."

"Life is full of other people's mistakes."

Lil pointed to the navy cap she had worn out of the house when her mother wasn't looking. "That's a real

USN hat. My cousin gave it to me. He joined the navy."

"I'm impressed," the woman said. "But if you're smart, you'll let me keep it for you till the end of the day."

Lil frowned. "I want people to see it."

The woman had very direct blue eyes. "If you were the princess of Kashmir and you possessed the sacred pearl of the East, would you wear it out among the crowds in the street?"

"Not unless I had rocks in my head."

The woman waited a moment. "Unless you want that real, genuine USN cap snatched off your head by some giant of a boy at recess, I suggest you leave it with me."

"Oh." Lil made the connection with the princess of Kashmir. "Will you lock it up?"

"I will."

"Well, all right. But don't let the key out of your possession."

"Don't worry. How is the bump on your head?" She glanced past Lil at two students who had just come into the office.

She's changing the subject, Lil thought, so those kids won't catch on. Pretty smart. She folded the hat and slid it across the counter to the clerk, who swept it into a drawer.

"Better, thank you. I'll have a scar, though."

The woman gave a little bark of sound that seemed to be meant as a laugh. "Don't look so pleased about it." She handed Lil her admittance slip. "Fifth grade is right next to fourth." She turned away to take care of the next child in line.

Lil went upstairs carrying her new lunch box. Her mother had bought it for her after Jay's mother said she always let Jay take his lunch. "There's no point," Mrs. Collier had said, "having them underfoot at noon when we don't need to." She hadn't meant Lil to hear, but Lil had heard. When her mother translated it for Lil's father, it was phrased differently: "It's too much of a strain for Lil to have to rush home at noon and back again, when Mary could fix her a nice nutritious lunch."

He had made some mild objection about the value of a hot meal, but his wife overruled him.

"You have a nice egg salad sandwich," her mother had told her this morning, "and an apple and two raisin cookies. Now I want you to go to that little store that Mr. Durant has . . ."

"I can't go off the schoolgrounds if I don't go home," Lil said.

"You don't have to go off the schoolgrounds. His house is right on the property line, and he has his store in his back hall. I want you to go there and get a small bottle of milk. No Moxie, no sarsaparilla, mind you, but *milk.*"

"And stay off that Coca-Cola stuff," Mary said. "It's full of cocaine."

"Oh, Mary," Lil's mother said, "I'm sure it isn't."

"Stuffed with it. Cocaine and caffeine and nicotine and only the saints know what else," Mary said.

"How do the saints know?" Lil asked, faking innocence. "Do they dope up on it?"

Mary took a wild swing at her. "Get along with you. You're going to be late to school, and they'll tan your hide."

But Lil had not been late. The bell was ringing as she went into the fifth grade. She was nervous, but not quite as much as she had been on the first day. At least everybody knew she was smart enough to skip a grade. And she still had a strip of adhesive plaster over her wound. She had combed her hair carefully so that the plaster would show.

"Good morning, you must be Lillian." This teacher was tall and broad and she looked about a hundred years old to Lillian, except that she had very expressive eyes.

"Yes, I am," Lillian said. She was conscious of the eighteen pairs of eyes staring at her. The nineteenth pair belonged to Jay, who was pretending that there was no girl named Lillian G. Adams standing in front of the teacher's desk. He was gazing fixedly out the window.

"I'm Mrs. Mason," the teacher said. "Your seat is over there in the second row, three seats back."

Mrs. Mason was very brisk, and Lillian realized that any thought she might have had of putting anything over on her at any time was a pipe dream. Jay had said Mrs. Mason had eyes in the back of her head. Lil had scoffed, but now she was ready to believe it as she saw Mrs. Mason point an accusing finger at a boy who had just sailed a paper airplane through the air, completely out of her line of vision.

Lil settled herself in her seat and put her lunch box and her pencils and paper inside the battered desk. She saw at once that the despised Tootie Gallagher, who was always trying to horn in on the games Lil and Jay played, was two seats behind her.

Tootie was glaring at her with her small, unfriendly eyes. Everything about Tootie was short and square, her body, her face, her haircut, even her nose.

"Tootie is mad because I'm in her grade," Lil thought with pleasure. "I've probably ruined her year."

Mrs. Mason called the roll, and they all stood to salute the flag that hung limply at one side of the blackboard.

As soon as the ragged chorus of "liberty and justice

for all" had died away, Mrs. Mason attacked fractions.

Lil had to pay close attention because her tutor last year had only just begun fractions before they moved away, and she did not understand them at all. Mrs. Mason glanced at her from time to time to see if she was following but didn't call on her. Tootie Gallagher shone in fractions, and Jay did pretty well, too, but there were quite a few pupils who didn't seem to know any more about them than Lil did. That was small comfort, however; she didn't intend to be one of those mediocre people. She wanted to be outstanding. She wanted to outshine Tootie Gallagher.

American history was better. Lil knew a lot about American history, because when she was sick, she had read a lot of books. She impressed Mrs. Mason by speaking up about Shays' Rebellion, which was not even in the textbook. In fact, she talked so much about Shays' Rebellion that Johnny Ash, who sat next to Lil, began yawning widely, and Jay started staring out the window again so nobody would think he knew her.

"That's very good, Lillian," Mrs. Mason said. "You must read a lot."

"Oh, I do," Lil said.

"But I think we'd better get on. Who can tell me what great event took place in 1787?"

"Con-sti-tu-tional Con-ven-tion." It was a chorus of

voices, but Tootie Gallagher's was the loudest, and she was waving her hand in hard, frantic pumping motions.

"All right, Doris, you tell us about the Constitutional Convention."

It took Lil a moment to realize that "Doris" was Tootie.

Tootie leaped to her feet and reeled off the details of the Constitutional Convention until Mrs. Mason managed to thank her and sit her down.

"Well," Mrs. Mason said, smoothing down the wiry hair that tended to spring around her face, "I am very gratified to have a class that is going to do its homework this year." She sat down as if to catch her breath.

Poor woman, Lil thought; she ought to be in a nice, comfortable wheelchair somewhere, sitting in the sun.

At recess Lil hung around the edges of groups, not knowing what to do with herself. Some of the kids congregated in Mr. Durant's store, but her mother had given her just enough money, one nickel, for a bottle of milk, and Lil knew she'd catch it if she spent that money for anything else. She would have to start saving some of her allowance for Mr. Durant's goodies.

She watched some girls playing snap-the-whip until she saw Tootie Gallagher leave the line and come toward her. She made herself scarce. It wasn't hard to tell what Tootie was up to. She was going to ask Lil to play, and then they'd put Lil on the end of the line and snap her off. She had fallen for that trick once, in the Boston school, and once was enough.

"I have to go to the girls' room," she said, when Tootie got near enough, and she ran for the schoolhouse before Tootie could say a word.

After recess they had spelling, and Lil beat out not only Tootie but Jay and a boy named Charlie, with the word "anaesthetic."

"It's not fair," Tootie said. "Her father's a doctor."

Mrs. Mason laughed, for the first time that morning. "I don't suppose, Doris, that Lillian and her parents sit down at the supper table and spell words like *anaesthetic* . . . or for that matter, *analgesic* or *ptomaine*."

But Tootie grumbled for a long time.

At lunchtime Tootie was unexpectedly nice. She sat with Lil while they ate their lunches on the wide stone steps that led to the girls' entrance. She pointed out different people and told Lil who they were.

"That's Myrna." She pointed to a tall, older girl standing by the fence, facing a line of half a dozen girls, most of them first or second graders. She was taking each child by the arm, doing something to the arm, and then giving the child something.

"What's she doing? Who is she?"

"She's initiating new kids into the Shifters." Tootie said it in a low, conspiratorial voice.

"What's Shifters?"

Tootie hesitated. "Well, since we're friends, I'll tell you. It's a special secret society. It might be connected to the military, but I'm not sure."

"Do you belong?"

"Oh, sure. For a couple years now."

"What do they do?"

"Oh, I can't tell."

Lil hated secrets that she wasn't in on. "I don't think it's anything."

"Well, you can see with your own eyes." Tootie pointed as Myrna pinned something to a little girl's sweater. "If you're not a Shifter, you're nobody, around here."

"I'm only interested in efforts to win the war," Lillian said loftily. "We have to beat the kaiser."

Tootie shrugged and got up. "Myrna probably wouldn't let you in anyway."

"Why not!" Lillian jumped up, spilling cookie crumbs.

Tootie looked her over. "We don't really know anything about you. Every stranger is a possible spy. It said so on the radio."

"Spy! me?" Lil felt her face burn with indignation. "My own first cousin is on a secret mission for the U.S. Navy right now."

"Well . . ." Tootie pretended to think it over. "I'll see what Myrna says." She ran over to the line and whispered in Myrna's ear. Myrna, who had a wild, shaggy head of yellow hair, shook her off as if she were a mosquito.

Tootie came back. "She says you can join, but hurry up." She dragged Lil over to the line and pushed her in ahead of some of the younger ones, who protested, but very quietly.

Tootie ran off. Lil looked at the child in front of her. "Why are you joining?"

The child shrugged. "They told me to."

"Who?"

"Kids."

Lil's doubts were returning. She didn't trust Tootie worth a plugged nickel. And she was the only kid older than six or seven in this line. She leaned forward, trying to see what Myrna did to the new members, and what she said.

She didn't seem to say anything, and what she did was very odd. She shoved up each girl's sleeve and made a light jab at the arm with a large safety pin. Then she pinned something that looked like one of those snap-together paper clips to the girl's blouse or sweater.

"That's not sanitary," Lillian said, looking at the rusty safety pin.

But Myrna had already disposed of the little girl in front of Lil and was pulling Lil toward her with an iron grip.

"Hey!" Lil said. "I changed my mind." But Myrna, who never looked up, never changed expression, was already rolling up Lil's sleeve and jabbing her with the pin.

"Ouch!" Lil said as Myrna snapped the Shifters pin onto her collar and pushed her out of the way for the next initiate.

Lil looked at a couple of the children who had gone ahead of her. "Is that all?" she said. "Aren't there any vows or passwords?"

A second grader, wise in her second-year sophistication, said, "Aw, it's just another vaccination."

It was a hoax, that's what it was. Lil didn't know what Myrna's motive was, but she knew Tootie's. Tootie had wanted to make a fool of her, and she had. She looked around, ready for a fight, but Tootie was not in sight.

One of the teachers came hurrying across the school yard, calling, "Girls! Girls!"

At the sound of her voice Myrna threw away the safety pin, sprang over the fence, and disappeared. The children stood around looking bewildered.

Lillian kept as far away from them as she could, but as the bell rang and the teacher was herding the group toward the door, she was saying, "Report to the nurse's office, all of you. Good heavens, you could get blood poisoning." She seemed very upset. "That girl ought to be in Danvers."

Lillian looked at the scratch on her arm and saw two tiny drops of blood. If she got blood poisoning and died, her father could sue Tootie and have her sent to jail. Or Danvers. That was where they put crazy people, and her father said it was a disgrace to society. Somewhere that was a disgrace to society would be just the place for Tootie.

In civics class Tootie looked up and gave her an angelic smile.

"I'll get you for that," Lil muttered.

"Lillian Adams." Mrs. Mason rapped her pointer against the blackboard. "One more word and you'll have to stay after. And do stop scowling so. You look like the kaiser himself."

"I noticed the resemblance," Tootie piped up.

"Doris! Fold your hands and button your lip."

That made Lil feel a little better.

"Now, we're ready for our patriotism talks." Mrs. Mason leaned against the blackboard, which she shouldn't have done because it made gray, chalky marks all over her black blouse, which didn't look too good to begin with. Mrs. Mason was not a snappy dresser. Ernie said a woman should be a snappy dresser at all times.

Her mind wandered as Harriet Nikopolus spoke in

a nasal monotone about the importance of knitting helmet liners and scarves, saving peach pits to be ground into charcoal to use as filters in gas masks. . . . Lil's mind left Harriet altogether and concentrated on Ernie. At least they couldn't use gas against our boys in the middle of the ocean. There were submarines, though. Since Ernie left she had been reading the war news in her father's newspaper. It seemed as if a German U-boat attacked an American or British ship nearly every day. The Russian czars had been kicked out; the Germans were all over the place, even Africa. Patriotism was all well and good, but Lil wished Ernie hadn't been in such a hurry. He couldn't win the war all by himself, and he ought to be home going to vocational school and riding his Harley-Davidson and marrying Mary. He was only seventeen, for heaven's sake.

Lillian woke up to the fact that Harriet was sitting down and being praised by Mrs. Mason for her speech.

"And now, Lillian," Mrs. Mason said, "we'll have your talk."

Lillian was startled. Jay had told her about the speeches and other homework, but this was her first day. She hadn't expected to be called on till tomorrow at the earliest. And she hadn't prepared a thing. But she couldn't admit that. Certainly she could ad-lib a speech about patriotism that would be better than Harriet's. After all, with her own first cousin a hero in the navy, she had something real to speak from, even if she couldn't divulge any state secrets. *Not* divulging state secrets . . . she'd use that for her theme.

She moved to the front of the room, remembering to take her hands out of her pockets because her mother said it made her look like a tomboy.

"The title of my speech," she said, "Is 'Spies and Lies.'" She glanced around the room at the faces and saw that they were interested. She'd scare these kids so bad they wouldn't sleep for a week. "Have you given a thought," she said in a ringing voice, "to the people you pass on the street every day? You think you know them, but do you? Did Julius Caesar know Brutus?" (That ought to go over big with Mrs. Mason.) "Did George Washington know Benedict Arnold? They-only-thought-they-did." She gave heavy emphasis to each word. "Think about this for a minute: You may be saying hi to a spy!"

She could hear some of them catch their breath. They were impressed. She lowered her voice to a more threatening pitch. "Consider the man who lives just down the street. You've known him all your life. But have you *really known him*?" She paused. "And how are you to tell what kind of man it is who smiles and smiles and says, 'Isn't it a lovely day?' Well, I'll tell you some ways.

Does he go to the beach a lot? People don't go to the beach after summer is over unless it's for *some purpose*. If he goes to the beach, does he take a flashlight with him? If you follow the news as closely as I do, you know that U-boats have been sighted off our very own coast. Is this man you think of as an old friend down at the beach, signaling the enemy at night?"

She had them in the palm of her hand. Every eye was on her. No wonder her mother liked acting. It was great.

"Does some stranger passing through town stop for a cup of coffee and does he say, just offhand, 'We haven't got a chance of winning this war. The Huns have got it wrapped up'? Does he say, 'Our boys aren't ready for war. They look like little kids playing with toy boats, in those sailor suits. And those hats the doughboys wear . . . what a laugh'? Is that the way this stranger talks? Believe me, friends, these traitors and spies are everywhere!" Five minutes later she felt she was just getting into full stride, but Mrs. Mason signaled her to stop.

"It's a very spirited speech, Lillian," she said, "and I'm certainly proud of your fine patriotic zeal. It's an inspiration to us all. But I'm afraid the bell is about to ring, and I want to give you your homework. . . ." The bell interrupted her, but she kept them seated until she had given the assignment.

Lillian glanced around the room, trying not to be obvious about it. Almost everyone was looking at her, and all she could see in their faces was awe. Jay was looking at the ceiling and whistling softly as he shoved his books into his desk. Tootie was sitting slumped in her seat as if she had not heard the bell. She looked, Lil thought, defeated. It was a wonderful thing when you could get even with your enemies and serve your country all at the same time.

Chapter
SIX

◘¦◘¦◘¦◘¦◘¦◘¦◘¦◘

LIL'S SPEECH was such a success that Danny Moe, the smallest boy in the class, was afraid to walk home after school. Lil offered to escort him, and Mrs. Mason praised her for her sense of responsibility. It was not so much responsibility as a wish to get another look at Asbury Grove, where Danny lived. She had been there once with her father during the summer while the Methodist camp meeting was going on, and she had been wanting to go back.

Asbury Grove was a place at the edge of town with lots of tall pine trees, a couple of hundred summer cottages, a tabernacle, a chapel, and its own post office and grocery store. It had been a Methodist campground since before the Civil War.

"Do you go to camp meeting every day all summer?" Lil asked Danny. It was a hot afternoon and she was beginning to wish she hadn't come. Danny walked so close, he trod on her heels.

"Not since Mama died." Danny was very small for a fifth grader, and he had a high voice.

"Do you and your dad live there alone? All year?"

"Sure. Why bother moving?" He stepped on her heel again. "Do you really know a lot of spies?"

"Not personally. I didn't say I did."

"Jay said you knew a spy that had to crawl on the floor and kiss the flag."

"I just said I know who he is."

"Who is he?"

"I can't tell."

"Jay said you made it up. Did you make up the one that yells in German at kids and pours water on them?"

"Danny, I can't tell anybody but Washington, D.C."

Danny scurried along in worried silence. "Are you a spy if you're a Socialist?"

"Absolutely." She had read in the paper that the known Socialists were being closely watched. Also people in labor unions.

In a voice so small she could hardly hear him, he

said, "My father is a Socialist."

Lil was shocked. She had never known anyone who even knew a Socialist. She felt suddenly protective toward poor little Danny. "He probably isn't really. Sometimes people say they are something but they don't mean it. I knew a boy in Brookline who said he was a monkey. He used to hang from trees by his heels. But he wasn't really a monkey."

In the same faint voice Danny said, "I think my father is really a Socialist. He goes to meetings."

Lil was shaken. "Listen," she said, "don't worry. If they arrest him, we'll adopt you."

"I don't want him to get arrested. I like him. They won't tar and feather him, like you said, will they?"

"Of course not." But she sounded more certain than she felt. It had never occurred to her when she gave her rousing speech that there might be a child in the room whose parent was a spy. "Maybe all Socialists aren't spies," she said. "There are probably nice Socialists."

Danny didn't say any more. His silence depressed her even more than what he had said. She was relieved when they reached his cottage, just inside the arched entrance to the Grove, and he ran inside.

She felt like hurrying home, but on the other hand she was here in the Grove, and she did want to look around. It was silent and spooky at this time of year, with nearly all the cottagers gone. If you really were a spy, she thought, the Grove would probably be a good place to hide out. She wished she had asked Danny if he ever saw strange lights at night, or if his father ever mentioned U-boats. The papers said there had been rumors of German U-boats off the coast.

She walked over to the big open-air tabernacle and sat down on one of the semicircular benches. Her mother had said that some of the camp-meeting preachers "spoke blood and thunder." She stared at the dais at the front and in her mind she heard a roar of words; with them, a cloud of thin smoke seemed to rise into the trees. She shivered and looked around her. Sunlight filtered in patches through the tall pines, and the silence was loud in her ears.

Suddenly from somewhere nearby a high voice laughed, a long, shrill peal of laughter. Lil jumped to her feet and looked around. No one was in sight. The laugh came again, and a babble of words that she couldn't understand. She clambered over the wooden benches and ran.

The laughter echoed behind her as she fled from the Grove. She didn't stop running till she was halfway down Asbury Street and saw Tootie Gallagher on her bicycle coming toward her.

Tootie jerked to a stop in front of her. "What were you running for?"

"Exercise," Lil said shortly, trying to control her breathing.

"Jay said you took Danny Moe home."

"What of it?"

"I don't go to the Grove in the winter."

"It isn't winter yet."

"When there's nobody up there, you might run into . . . you know who." Tootie bared her teeth in a horrible grin.

Lil was dying to ask who, but she was not going to give Tootie the satisfaction. She walked along briskly, but Tootie rode beside her.

"You made all that up," Tootie said, "about spies. You copied it off government posters."

"I did not." Lil gave Tootie the kind of devastating stare that her mother gave her sometimes when she was angry.

"Everybody knew you were making it up, except old Mason. She'll swallow anything."

Lil tried to walk faster. Ignore the enemy. Let him waste his ammo on the empty air.

"There aren't any spies around here. If there were, we'd hound 'em right into the Charlestown jail, me and my gang."

"Your gang," Lil said, with withering scorn. "Ha! Ha!" She had to sidestep to keep from bumping into Tootie's bike. "Will you please get out of the way? I'm trying to walk home."

"Who's stopping you? You don't own this street. You're just a stranger here. Maybe *you're* a spy. Wait till I tell Myrna! She don't allow spies in the Shifters. Did your vaccination take? Lemme look." She grabbed Lil's arm.

Lil kicked out at the bike and it crashed on its side, Tootie with it. Lil ran down the road toward home with Tootie's howls of rage sounding in her ears.

Chapter
SEVEN

❘0❘0❘0❘0❘0❘0❘0❘0

IT WAS SOME TIME before the subject of Lil's talk on spies finally died away, the timid stopped asking questions, and the skeptics, egged on by Tootie, stopped trying to get her to admit she'd made it all up. She was thoroughly sick of the subject, even though Mrs. Mason gave her an A.

Instead, she tried to turn the conversation to Halloween, though it was still almost a month away. Her mother and Jay's had announced they were going to give a small party at Lil's house. However, Lil was not supposed to talk about that; Lil's mother was quite firm about it.

She still remembered the year she had promised Lil a "small party," and Lil had showed up with the entire first grade.

So she talked instead about the tricks they would play. Jay and Charlie had their hearts set on overturning some of the outhouses still in use on farms at the edge of town. Lil thought that was a revolting idea, but she was all in favor of ringing people's doorbells, writing in soap on windows, and appearing in terrifying costumes.

At dinner one night Lil pestered her mother about a costume. "Something bloodcurdling," she said.

"Ask Mary," her mother said. "I can't think of anything but the Mothers' Club show. I can't think why they asked me to direct it."

"Because if they hadn't," her husband said, "you wouldn't have spoken to them for a month. Besides, you're a pro, old girl."

"About my costume," Lil said, turning to Mary. She was not interested in the Mothers' Club show. She had seen amateur local talent shows before; her mother was always starring in them or directing or both. Lil found it embarrassing.

"Don't look at me," Mary said. "In the old country we didn't play fast and loose with spirits. Besides, I have to think up food for your party. Fricasseed bats' wings, I suppose."

"To change the subject," Lil's father said, "this is a

splendid steak. Who did you wangle it from? I haven't seen good beef since the war began."

"She makes eyes at Mr. Lomax," Lil said. Mr. Lomax was the butcher.

"The ghosts give it to me," Mary said. "Speakin' of ghosts, I saw that Myrna Smalley child today, and there's a walkin' ghost if ever there was one."

Lil stopped eating her steak to listen. She had hardly thought of Myrna since the day of the Shifters business, and now she realized that she hadn't seen her around either.

Her father shook his head. "Poor kid. She's getting out of hand, I'm afraid. If she were my patient, I'd talk to her people about an institution before she hurts herself. But they take her to Salem to the doctor."

"Who are you talking about?" Lil's mother said. "Lillian, eat your carrots. How do you expect to see at night if you don't eat your carrots?"

"The Smalley girl," Lil's father said. "She has spells."

Lillian had never told her family about the Shifters. It was not a subject she liked even to think about, let alone mention. She had let Tootie Gallagher make a fool of her. First graders couldn't be expected to realize that it was just a crazy stunt, but she should have known. "Is Myrna crazy?" she asked her father.

He frowned. "I don't like that word. People use it

to describe anyone who's different from themselves. Myrna doesn't see the world the way we do, and she needs help to keep from hurting herself, that's all."

"Like Crazy Harry," Mary said. Mary had had a letter from Ernie that day, after a week of silence, and she was in a very happy mood.

"That's exactly what I mean," Lil's father said. "Harry is a good man. When he was young, he went to Harvard. They say he was very bright and very handsome . . ."

Mary burst out laughing. "You're havin' me on!"

"No, that's what people who knew him say. He developed scarlet fever in his senior year, and it affected his brain. But he does nobody any harm, and he's an excellent fiddler."

Mary looked skeptical, but she said no more.

Lil knew the man they were talking about. The kids teased him sometimes, but they all liked him. He was a very tall man with shoulder-length gray hair and a long black coat that flapped around him when he walked. He was always laughing and talking to himself, and he always carried his fiddle under his arm. He had been all over the place on Labor Day, playing for the parade and the crowd.

"I was scared of Harry the first time I saw him," she said, "but he's really nice."

"Nice or not nice," Mary said, "crazy people are

crazy, and there's no two ways about it."

Lil was surprised at the stern look her father gave Mary. He liked her, and he usually defended her when she argued with Lil's mother.

"There but for the grace of God go all of us," he said, and Mary hastily crossed herself and said, "Amen."

"There are those who believe," he went on, "that the people who are called crazy are wiser than any of us."

"What do you think," Lil's mother said, not having really listened to the conversation, "about Mattie Spivak as a clown?"

Her husband laughed till he choked and had to leave the table.

Lil's mother looked puzzled. "What is he laughing at?"

After she went to bed that night, Lil thought about the conversation and wondered why her father had laughed. Maybe it was because Mattie Spivak was a very serious woman, the "best housekeeper in town," people said. Picturing Mrs. Spivak in a clown costume, Lil laughed, herself. It *was* funny. Maybe that was why her mother had thought of it—Mattie Spivak, the unclowniest woman in town. It would make everybody laugh.

That made her think about Crazy Harry; she wondered if he'd be a good person to pester on Halloween. No.

It wasn't any fun to haunt people who didn't mind, and she was sure Harry would not mind. He'd probably want to join them, with his long black cape flying and his hair streaming out behind him. Scary Harry, she thought, and laughed. He was no more scary than Mattie Spivak was clownish. Anyway, she didn't know where he lived.

In the morning she said to Mary, "Where does Crazy Harry live, anyway?" She was having second thoughts about him as a Halloween target, mainly because she needed to come up with some good suggestion. So far, Jay and Charlie and Tootie had had all the really great ideas.

"Up to the Grove," Mary said. "Lives all by himself in one of them Methodist cottages. They say he cooks his own meals, looks after himself. But he wanders around up there, talking and laughing at the top of his lungs. Your father may say what he likes, but crazy is crazy, in my opinion." She slapped a fried egg over and gave it a hard poke.

Lil waited a moment, and then she said, "The Grove?"

"Yes, the Grove. You want two biscuits or three?"

"Three." Lil sat down in the kitchen chair. The Grove? Laughter? A voice talking by itself? Could it have been Harry who scared her so, that day at Asbury Grove? And Tootie Gallagher probably knew it, she thought angrily; she saw me running down the road. She tried to remember what Tootie had said to her. She never went to the Grove except in summer, she had said; you might run into . . . And she hadn't finished. And she had laughed. Tootie knew! Once again Lil had made a fool of herself in front of Tootie Gallagher. She had been scared out of her wits by poor, harmless Crazy Harry. Somehow she had to get even with Tootie Gallagher, if it was the last thing she did.

Lil thought about it all day. Mrs. Mason had to call on her three times in history before she realized she'd been called on. At noon Jay and Charlie told her that maybe they didn't want to go with girls on Halloween anyway.

"You'll chicken out," Charlie said.

"I will not!"

They ignored her, putting their heads together over Mr. Durant's assortment of ice-cream bars. Lil ignored *them*, concentrating on candy bars, but it was not really satisfactory to ignore somebody who was already ignoring you.

After she had paid Mr. Durant her nickel, she said, "I'm probably going to have a dinosaur costume for Halloween."

"What's a dinosaur costume?" Charlie said. He was a thin boy with glasses, and Lil thought he was not very bright, although he always did well in spelling. He seemed to think he owned Jay.

"A dinosaur is an ancient extinct animal," she said, trying to sound superior like Mrs. Mason, "and it was very scary."

"How can anybody be scared of something that's been dead for thousands of millions of years?" Tootie said. "I'm going to be a pirate, myself. With one eye and a wooden leg."

"I suppose you're going to cut off your leg just for Halloween," Lil said, but she could see that Charlie and Jay were impressed with the pirate idea.

"You could wear a patch," Jay said. "On your eye. I could lend you my grandfather's crutch."

Lil felt betrayed. She watched the three of them walk away together, ignoring her. She didn't care. Maybe she wouldn't even go out on Halloween. It was childish anyway. Maybe she was getting too old for that stuff.

She did badly on the fractions test that afternoon, and Mrs. Mason scolded her for not applying herself.

"Well, it's a beauty of a mood you're in," Mary said to her when she slammed into the kitchen after school.

"Never mind!" Lil said crossly. And she added, "Maybe I'm going to be sick."

"Sick, my foot. Who did you dirt at school today?"

"Nobody," Lil said. She grabbed some cookies from the blue jar. "I hate those kids. I wouldn't be bothered talking to them."

"Not much," Mary said. Her hands were white with

flour from the bread she was making. "Well, pay them no mind, dearie. They're just a bunch of kids."

As Lil was leaving the kitchen, Mary said, "Your ma left you a note, some errands she wants done."

"Blast her eyes!" Lil said, and Mary giggled.

Lil picked up the note. "Dear Lillian: I have to rehearse the clown act this afternoon. Please get a jar of molasses at the store, and leave my shoes with Mr. Panzi to be reheeled. Bring home the change from the molasses." There was a dollar bill folded under the note, and next to them was a pair of brown leather shoes with four buttons.

Lil grumbled as she walked down the street. I sound like Crazy Harry, she thought, talking to myself. Maybe it made him feel better to talk to himself. He didn't seem to mind when people teased him. There must be something left of that part of his brain that was so smart before he got sick, something telling him not to worry.

Thinking of Crazy Harry reminded her of Danny Moe. She wondered if anyone had found out that Mr. Moe was a Socialist. She didn't really think he was a spy. Of course if he was, and she reported him, she'd get a medal and her name in the papers. But then she thought of how Danny would feel, and she decided it wouldn't be worth it.

She went into the grocery store and bought the molasses

from Bernie Monroe, who was in high school. He said somebody told him she made a good war speech about spies.

"That was quite a while ago," she said, blushing.

"Did you read in the papers about spies poisoning Red Cross bandages?"

She was shocked. Then she decided he might be teasing her. "I hadn't heard about that." She hoped she sounded impressed, in case he was serious, and wise to his joke if he was teasing. What a terrible thing to do, if it was true! It made her shiver all over to think of wounded soldiers and sailors suffering like that. Oh, she wished they'd send Ernie home.

Reluctantly she pushed open the door to the shoemaker's shop with her toe and entered cautiously. For all she knew, he might be ready to dump a bucket of water on her. But the shop seemed to be empty.

On the counter there was a glass jar half full of peach pits and a hand-lettered sign that said Save Pits for Our Boys. Maybe he was a patriot after all. On the other hand maybe that was just a cover-up, to fool people. Mrs. Mason had quoted some big writer who said traitors wrap themselves in the flag. Maybe Mr. Panzi wrapped himself in a peach pit. The idea made her giggle.

Well, she couldn't stand there all day. She looked around for a pencil and scrap of paper so she could write "Please reheel for Mrs. Adams," but she couldn't find anything. Maybe she'd have to come back. She looked around at the shelves with pairs of shoes tagged neatly.

It occurred to her that if she could think of some new way to torment Mr. Panzi on Halloween, the other kids might listen to her. All they ever did was bang on his door till he chased them. There must be some better way to torment him.

She jumped as Mr. Panzi loomed up in the small doorway that opened into the back of the shop, where the shoemaking equipment was.

He grabbed the shoes from her hand and slammed them on the counter. "What you want dese shoes?" he demanded.

"Reheel," Lil said faintly.

He thrust a ticket for the shoes into her hand and shooed her toward the door. "Nex' veek Tuesday."

She dropped her mother's change but she didn't stop to pick it up. She ran all the way home, and when she got there, she found Mary sobbing in the kitchen, with a letter clutched in her hand.

"He's gone," Mary cried at her.

"Who's gone?"

"Himself. Gone to sea in a mystery ship, can't even write. He'll be killed; oh, he'll be killed deader'n a doornail!"

Lil's heart sank. If anything happened to Ernie, she did not think she could stand it. "Stop crying," she said. She shook Mary's arm. "Nothing ever happens to Ernie. If you don't stop crying, you'll *make* something bad happen."

Mary gasped and struggled to control her sobs. Then she grabbed a hat from the back hall hook. "I'm goin' to church," she said. "I'm goin' to pray for his immortal soul."

Lil sat on the back steps feeling as if she were no bigger than the ant that was scurrying back and forth near her foot. She was helpless. There was nothing she could do.

"God," she said aloud, "take care of him."

Suddenly Jay flew into the yard on his bike. "You want to play trench warfare?" he demanded. "We haven't got enough kids."

Lillian sighed. There was nothing else to do. She might as well play trench warfare. But her heart was not in it.

Chapter
EIGHT

0:0:0:0:0:0:0:0

HER MOTHER's grim insistence that Ernie was going to be just fine worried Lil more than Mary's crying spells. Every day Lil pored over the casualty lists in the paper, and she glued little colored scraps of paper to her world globe to show where the Germans were. She knew the U-boats had sunk eight million tons of Allied shipping, and that Ernie was probably on one of the destroyers that were accompanying U.S. ships, although that was just a guess on her father's part.

When the Germans invaded Portuguese East Africa,

she asked Mrs. Mason where it was; she was never sure about the different parts of Africa. Mrs. Mason gave the class a geography lesson right then. A few days later Lil gave a report on the execution of the woman spy Mata Hari.

"You got spies on the brain," Tootie Gallagher said, and the rest of the class laughed.

After school she tripped Tootie Gallagher and made her drop all her books. Tootie chased her, but Lil could run faster.

The truth was she had thought a lot about Mata Hari. She wondered if she had been hanged or shot or what. A spy like that should be shot, all right, but it would hurt, even if you were a German. She wondered if Mata Hari was beautiful, as the papers said, or if she was just a homely little twerp like Tootie Gallagher.

Danny Moe always defended Lil, no matter what she said or did. Sometimes she walked to the Grove with him, partly in the hope of seeing his father, partly to see Crazy Harry. The day she tripped Tootie, he caught up with her and they walked single file along the streetcar rails, trying to see who could go the longest without stepping off. Danny won, but he said he had more practice; he walked the rails nearly every day on his way to school.

"Danny," she said, "do you know Crazy Harry well?"

"Oh, sure. I see him a lot. Sometimes he gives me

cookies. He bakes cookies just for fun. They aren't very good, but I eat them. I wish people didn't call him crazy."

"My father says maybe the people they call crazy are the ones who aren't."

Danny thought about that for a minute. "That's nice. I like that."

They walked along a little further. "Danny, is your dad . . . you know . . . is he all right? No trouble or anything?"

Danny frowned worriedly. "No, he's all right. He still goes to meetings, though. He thinks it's a rotten war."

"That's unpatriotic," Lil said.

"Well, he loves the United States. He just thinks everybody's getting killed in a dumb fight over territory that doesn't have anything to do with America."

Lil stuck her hands in the pockets of her skirt and walked along in silence. Her own father had made some remarks not too different from that. Her mother had given him a talking-to about getting into trouble. It was very puzzling to her that someone like her father, and Mary, too, and now Danny's father, could have such dangerous views. She wished she could talk to somebody about it.

She had had a question in mind ever since the day she went to the shoemaker's. How did you really tell a spy? She was pretty sure that Mr. Panzi was a German sympathizer. He was a foreigner, wasn't he? He spoke some crazy language that sounded like German; she had heard him. And he hated people. How could she prove he was a spy? And would people believe her if she could prove it?

She wondered if Crazy Harry could help. He must know Mr. Panzi, because Harry had lived here all his life. And since he was not like other grown-ups, he might see things more clearly; he might give her real answers.

"Do you think Harry would talk to me?" she asked.

"Sure," Danny said, "I'll find Harry for you if you want. I know the places he goes. Most people don't know."

Then he added, almost as an afterthought, "Can I go with you on Halloween?"

She knew Danny was bribing her, and she was willing to go for it, although she did have an uneasy feeling that she might get into trouble with the government of the United States if she got too friendly with the son of a Socialist. Just yesterday she had read in the *Boston Transcript* that the head of the Committee on Public Information said that trade-union men, Socialists, feminists, and pro-British people were likely to be spies. She didn't understand the British part, since they were America's allies, but who was she to question the government? "Your father isn't English, is he?" she said.

Danny looked surprised. "He was born in Topsfield. Why?"

She didn't answer his question, but she said, "I'll see, about Halloween."

He looked as happy as if she had said yes. He picked up a pinecone as they walked into the Grove and flung it at a squirrel. "My dad joined the Home Guard yesterday."

Lillian was amazed. "Why didn't you say so?" That had to prove he was a patriot, didn't it? Unless he had joined to find out the Guard's secrets. She doubted that the Home Guard had any secrets, though.

"He bought an old Ford so he can get home from work and get to the drills on time. He's going to teach me to drive it."

Lil's mind was working busily. The Guard drilled on Tuesday evenings. If she could get a good look at Mr. Moe, she might be able to tell what kind of person he was. "Do you want me to go with you to watch them drill next Tuesday?" she asked.

Danny gave a little leap of joy. "Yeah! Will ya?"

"I'll meet you there at six. It's our patriotic duty," she added piously, "to give them moral support."

As if wanting to make her as happy as he was, Danny

said, "You want to know how to turn your dog green?"

"I don't have a dog. And nobody can turn a dog green."

"I can. I'll tell you the trick. You get two pounds of capers at Jack Archer's father's fruit store, and you pound 'em good. Then you distill it . . ."

"What's distill mean?"

"You know, kind of steam it, so it vaporizes. Then you pour out what water's left . . ."

"You didn't say anything about water."

Patiently he said, "It won't steam without water. Anyway you put more water in and do it again. Then you wash the dog in that water, and he'll be green." He rocked back on his heels, looking pleased.

"I don't believe it."

"Honest. You try it."

"I don't have a dog."

"Jay has. It's a white dog. It'd look good green."

"Well." Lil was definitely interested. If it worked, she'd have something on Jay, all right. His mother would be mad, and she'd think Jay had done it. He said she always blamed him for everything. "Maybe I'll try it. How much do capers cost?"

"Oh, a dime a pound, I guess." They had arrived at Danny's cottage. "You want to come in?"

"What for?" Lillian felt nervous about going

into a Socialist's house. If anybody from the Committee saw her coming out, they might think she was a Socialist, too.

"I'll show you my uncle's picture. He's in a hospital in France. He's with the Fifth Marine Regiment, Second Division, only he got shot through the heel."

This was a very confusing family. A Socialist father and a Marine hero uncle? She decided to go in. If anybody saw her, she could say she was just making sure that Danny had enough to eat, since he had no mother or anything. She had heard her father say that a lot of kids were going hungry.

It was a very neat house without much furniture. Right away she saw a big picture of a pretty woman, who must be Danny's mother because she looked like him. She didn't like to ask, in case it would make him sad.

Proudly Danny brought an enlarged snapshot of a young man standing stiffly in his dress blues.

"He looks nice," Lil said. She wished desperately that she had a picture of Ernie in his uniform.

Danny got another smaller snapshot of the same man posed with two other Marines in their field uniforms, arms around each other, serious expressions on their faces. "That's before he got shot in the heel," Danny said. "That fellow there, on his left, that's his buddy Joe. Joe got killed by shell fire."

Lil stared at the picture for several minutes, especially at the long-jawed, determined face of Joe. It was very hard to imagine someone dead, when they looked so alive.

"He don't look a bit dead, does he?" Danny said softly.

"What did your father think when he heard Joe was killed?"

"He cried," Danny said.

Lil frowned. Danny's father was too much for her; she couldn't understand him at all. "Why did he cry?"

"Well, Joe was here a couple of times, before him and Uncle Pete went overseas. Joe and my dad got along like a house afire. They played chess practically one whole night."

Lil gave the picture back to Danny. She didn't want to hear any more about Joe. "Well, Ernie isn't going to get killed."

"Who's Ernie? Is he your uncle?"

"He's my best cousin. He's in the navy, somewhere on a mystery ship. We can't even write to him."

"I wouldn't like that," Danny said. "I write to Uncle Pete every week."

"Your uncle is safe in the hospital. My cousin Ernie is on the high seas. It's very dangerous. Only nothing will happen to Ernie. He lives a charmed life."

"That's good." He put the pictures back on the table. "I hope Uncle Pete's heel is bad enough so he don't get back in the front lines. I think no-man's-land must be real scary. There's barbed wire all over, and Germans throwing bombs at them. They have to live in the mud in dugouts and sometimes they don't get anything to eat. They get gassed sometimes."

Lil didn't want to hear any more about it. "Let's go find Crazy Harry."

"All right, but don't call him that to his face, will you? It hurts his feelings."

" 'Course I won't."

They walked deep into the Grove, looking for Harry.

"One time," Danny said, "Uncle Pete was carrying a mandolin for a buddy of his, had it strapped to his pack, and he got so tired he fell backward into a shell hole and smashed that mandolin all to pieces."

"Mandolin? What was he doing with a mandolin?"

"They'd play it when there was a chance." Danny opened the big wooden door to the chapel. "Sometimes Harry sits in here and thinks." But the chapel was empty.

It was a gray day with a chilly wind, and Lil was beginning to think that finding Harry was more trouble than it was worth. They had gone up and down the right-angled streets, past dozens of boarded-up cottages, but no Harry was in sight. The wind moaned in the pines, and she was getting hungry.

"Maybe I better go home. Mary'll be expecting me. She might make me some cocoa if she's in a good mood."

"Is Mary your mother?"

"No, she's our maid and my best friend. Except Ernie. She and Ernie are going to get married after the war."

"That's nice." Danny looked wistful. "My dad makes good cocoa, but he don't get home till a quarter of six. He works at the Shoe."

Lil knew about the Shoe—the United Shoe Machinery company in Beverly—where a lot of the local men worked. Her father said it was a sweatshop.

"Listen!" Danny grabbed Lillian's arm, his face lighting up.

The faint sound of violin music came to them.

"That's him. That's Harry playing his fiddle. Come on." He ran toward the open-air tabernacle.

Harry was standing on the small stage, his long hair blowing in the wind, playing his violin, his body swaying with the music and his face alight. Danny and Lil crept into the front row and sat down. Harry didn't seem to notice them.

He was playing a wild, gypsy-sounding song, and when he got to the end, he bowed low from the waist and held out his arms to his imaginary audience. Danny started to clap, and after a moment Lil joined in. Harry gave them a special bow.

"Thank you, ladies and gentlemen," he said in his

high voice, "thank you, thank you. I am happy to bring you my humble music." He cupped one hand behind his ear. "Encore? Do I hear a cry for encores? Well, thank you, I'd be proud." With a flourish, he began to play another song.

It was unlike any music Lil had ever heard, wild and sweet and sad all at once. It stirred feelings in her that she didn't understand. One minute she felt like dancing; the next minute she felt tears sting her eyes. She had the strange idea that if she could just understand what he was playing, she wouldn't have to ask him any questions.

When he finished and acknowledged the applause, he said, "Do I hear any requests?"

Lil got up and walked close to the stage, where she could look up at him. "Do you know any songs about the war, Mr. Harry?"

He scratched his head and gazed over her head for a moment. Then he said, "I believe I do, Madam." And he began to play and sing:

Lord Guthrie went off to the war, he did,
With his pack on his back, and he never came back.
He left his fair maid with her heart nearly broke,
For his valor was strong, was strong, was strong.
For his valor was strong, but he never came back.
Oh, weep for good Lord Guthrie.

He repeated the words and ended with a set of slow, almost discordant bars that sounded funereal.

Lil swallowed hard. "Thank you very much," she said.

"And now ladies, gentlemen, I must go. I have other concerts to give. Thank you for your appreciation."

"Well, he's gone," Danny said, as Harry pranced off into the woods. "Sometimes when he's giving a concert, he don't feel like talking."

"That's all right." Lil felt unsettled. She couldn't sort out her feelings, and that always troubled her. She liked to know what she thought at all times. "I got to go now."

"All right."

Lil started off and then stopped to look back at him. "You can come with us on Halloween if you want. Come to my house first. I'm having a party."

His face lit up. "Thanks!"

"You'll have to have a costume."

"I'll be a ghost."

A ghost wasn't very original. He'd probably just drape a sheet over himself. "I've got a big tin jack-o'-lantern you can wear on top of your head, if you want. It's got a big open space at the bottom so it'll fit if your head isn't too big."

"Thanks," Danny said. "Thanks a lot, Lil."

When she got home, Mary made cocoa. "Tomorrow

night's the show," she said. "Your mother's show. They say it's pretty good. You and your dad and me's got front-row seats." She sighed. "Ernie'd love to see it. He's that proud of your ma. And it's got a patriotic theme, she says. Well, I'll write him all about it."

"How can you write him? I thought we didn't know where he is."

"We don't. I write him every day anyway and save it for when he gets home. Then he'll know everything that's happened while he was gone."

He won't know everything, Lil thought. He won't know about Danny's Uncle Pete and about Joe, and I could never tell about Harry's concert. She wished she knew what it was she had learned from Harry. She couldn't put her finger on it. The funny thing was, she hadn't asked him anything.

Well, she had something else to think about tonight. Her father had bought her an almost-new bicycle from the Appleton boy, who had joined the Marines. Tomorrow it would arrive.

Chapter
NINE

0:0:0:0:0:0:0:0

"SAY, YOU got a new bike there, Lil?" It was Alec, the young blacksmith, who asked her. She had been riding all over town, and she had slowed down to watch him working at his forge with sparks flying around his head. He always seemed like someone out of Greek mythology, big and heavy-muscled in his leather apron, wielding his hammer in a halo of fire.

"It was Paul Appleton's. He's gone with the Marines."

He wiped his hands on his apron and came to look at it. "I remember. Took a little dent out of the fender for him, right after he got it. He rode it into the back of the hayrick. Nice boy, Paul." He smoothed the fender. "I ought to be over there myself, but who's going to shoe the horses in this town, I ask you?"

She knew he wasn't really asking her. Her father was in the same situation: Some people had to stay home to take care of what they were expert in. This town had hundreds of horses, both working and pleasure horses, and old Jasper Hyde, the other smithy, had died last winter.

"Well, don't run into any hayricks," Alec said. He tapped the silver handlebars with his blackened knuckles. "D'ya mind riding a boy's bike?" He had a faint Scottish accent.

"No, I've always hated girls' bikes."

Alec laughed. "Say good-day to Mary for me." He went back to work.

He had taken Mary to the movies a few times before she decided it wasn't fair to Ernie. They were still good friends.

At the end of the street she saw Jay heading north at full speed on his bike, with Tootie not far behind him.

Alec said, "They're chasing Charlie Davis. He just went by."

"Bye, Alec." She took off after them.

If they were chasing Charlie, they were probably heading for the Ward estate, where Janice of the pony cart lived. Charlie's father was head groom. Usually Lil liked to go with them, to hang around the stables.

She caught up with Tootie at a curve in the road. Tootie had skidded on the gravel and almost crashed into one of the huge elms that made an arch over the road. She had stopped to get her balance. When she saw Lil, she glared.

"Having a little trouble?" Lil asked with fake sympathy.

"Go to the devil," Tootie growled.

"Just wanted to be of assistance."

"Where'd you get that cheap secondhand bike?" Tootie said.

"None of your business." Now Lil was angry. It was not a cheap bike. It even had a headlamp.

"Well, don't trail after us. We don't want you." Tootie mounted her bike and rode off.

For a moment Lil was tempted to chase her and try to tip her over, but suddenly she decided it was too much trouble.

She turned back, riding in big loops from one side of the road to the other.

She wondered if Tootie would be at the Mothers' Club show. She hoped not. Tootie might laugh in all the wrong places. But she had said her brother was pulling the curtain, so it was pretty certain she'd be there. Lil's mother was worn out with all the rehearsing. Because of the war and the need to cheer people up, she wanted this show to be the best ever. Also, Lil suspected, it was because this was the first one here that her mother had had anything to do with. Last year they had been living in Brookline.

She circled in front of the hardware store and stopped, putting one foot on the curb to balance herself. Hot Dog came out, carrying a handful of shiny nails. He held them up. "Four cents. All those nails for four cents. Nails are cheap."

"Nice big ones." She wanted to say that Zack Pindar should have put them in a bag for him, but that would spoil Hot Dog's pleasure. He dropped one and then dropped another, trying to pick up the first one. She propped the bike pedal against the curb and got off to help him.

"Say, thanks." He beamed at her. "That's Paul Appleton's bike, ain't it?"

"It's mine now. My dad bought it for me."

"Paul's a Marine now." He said it with awe.

"I know."

"I wisht I was a Marine." He aimed a long, shiny nail. "Bam! Bam! I'd kill them krauts."

"Oh, Hot Dog, you wouldn't kill a fly."

"I would if I was mad enough. You get me mad and watch out." He lumbered up the street, every now and then dropping a nail, picking it up, aiming it, and saying, "Wham! Bam!"

Lil remembered she was supposed to get home early, to eat and to change her clothes for the show. Her mother was in her usual state of nerves. "I can't eat a bite of solid food," she always said before a show. She drank tea and nibbled at saltines.

John Kerrigan, assistant postmaster, came out of the post office. He was twenty-one but he couldn't fight in the war because he had asthma. Lil liked him. He was nice to everybody, even Fancy Pantsy. She'd seen him carry a heavy box from the post office to Pantsy's shop. Shoe leather, the box label said. Maybe it was really bombs.

"Nifty bike, Lil," he said.

She felt herself blush, which always made her mad. "Thanks," she said. "It was Paul Appleton's."

He looked wistful, and she wished she hadn't mentioned Paul. Tootie said she heard he cried when they told him he couldn't enlist.

"Looking forward to your mother's show," he said, smiling again.

She rode home slowly, watching John as he faded out of sight. She wished she were that nice.

She put her bike in the barn with great care, bracing it so it wouldn't fall over and dusting it off with an old rag Mary had given her.

When she went into the house, she found that her mother had already left for the Town Hall.

"It's not Broadway, New York," Mary grumbled as she got the supper on the table for Lil and her father and herself. Mary was not as happy as usual. There had been stories in the paper about U.S. destroyers being lost in the fight against the U-boats, and she was sure Ernie was gone forever.

She was in such a bad mood, she even tried to get Lil to wear a hair ribbon to the show. Lil finally appealed to her father. "Whoever sits behind me wouldn't be able to see," she said. "That stupid hair ribbon stands up a foot off my head."

He seemed tired, and she was glad he was going to get a night off. Mrs. Flaherty was coming to mind the phone while they were gone. "You know, Lil, I am about to come to the conclusion that you are too old for hair ribbons."

"Daddy!" She flew at him and hugged him. "Will you tell Mother?"

"I already have. A girl riding a bike at any considerable rate of speed, with a hair ribbon like the ones your mother creates, might very well sail off and be lost at sea." He meant to be funny, but the words "lost at sea" sent Mary into a fit of tears. He sighed. "Whoever said 'Least said, soonest mended' had the right idea. I'm sorry, Mary. My intuition tells me that Ernie is hale and hearty, and one of these days he will come bursting through that door, and you will all realize that I have second sight."

"Second sight indeed," Mary muttered.

"Well, it was a very good supper, and if you ladies will excuse me, I'll change into a clean shirt for the occasion."

Lil was wearing a new dress, light blue with dark blue flowers embroidered on the skirt. Wearing something new always made her self-conscious, but this time she was too nervous about her mother to think about how she looked. Mary brushed her hair so hard it hurt and grumbled about selfish children who wouldn't wear hair ribbons even to please their mother, who worked so hard for our boys. Since Mary usually was understanding about the ribbons, Lil knew she must be really upset.

"I'll wear that big barrette," she said. "That's almost as good as a hair ribbon, and people can see over it."

Mrs. Flaherty saw them off, saying, "Yes, Doctor, I know what you said. If it's somebody dyin' or havin' a baby, I'll call Town Hall and ask for youse."

Lil's father didn't entirely trust Mrs. Flaherty's judgment, but finally he and Mary and Lil drove off in the Buick touring car.

The long, semicircular drive in front of the Town Hall was already almost filled with cars and carriages. Horses were standing patiently, tied to the hitching rail. Lil saw Janice's pony cart. She wished she had thought to ask Danny Moe to come with them, although he might have felt shy about it. He was not much of a mixer with the other kids.

Mary, who was feeling better by the moment, said, "Would youse look at them gowns goin' in the door. Maybe it *is* Broadway, New York."

"Big-time stuff we got here," Lil's father said. He always teased Lil's mother a little about her stage career, although Lil knew he was proud of her. "Wouldn't be surprised if David Belasco showed up to look it over." He parked the Buick in what looked to be an impossibly small place. Lil thought he was the best driver in the world.

It took a while to get to their seats, so many people stopped her father to chat, but finally they were in the first row, in the center, and the curtain was about to go up. Only this curtain went sideways, parting in the middle, and Lil knew it was pulled by Johnny Gallagher, Tootie's fourteen-year-old brother.

The hall was buzzing with conversation. Jay and his

father sat right behind them, and Jay's dad and Lil's had a few jokes about opening-night nerves.

"Lucky for us," Jay's dad said, "opening night is also closing night. I don't know if I could stand it past the first performance."

Jay poked Lil's back. "I saw your bike."

"Where?" She was miffed that he had seen it before she had a chance to show it to him.

"Seen you going down Willow Street."

She waited for his judgmental remark. Finally it came. "It's not bad."

Tootie Gallagher, four rows back, signaled wildly, and Lil enjoyed the fact that she herself was the director's daughter and so had a front-row seat.

Other classmates scattered around the hall waved at her. She began to feel like a star herself.

"I suppose we've got to listen to Mel Wheeler do his four-minute-man spiel," her father said to Jay's father.

Lil wished her father wouldn't say those things in public. Mr. Wheeler was one of thousands of men around the country who were paid by the government to be four-minute men, to make a four-minute patriotic speech at public functions. She had heard him do his at the movie theater in Beverly. People had clapped and cheered when he talked about "our boys" and "Uncle Sam."

Lil saw Janice Ward come in with a very handsome second lieutenant. Some girls had all the luck—ponies and lieutenants . . .

Tootie Gallagher skidded down the aisle and stooped over Lil. "Did you see that officer Janice Ward is with?" she screeched in Lil's ear.

"I saw him, Doris," Lil said loftily.

"Isn't he gorgeous?"

"I'd rather have an ensign any day," Lil said.

Without warning the lights went out, and Lil chuckled as she heard Tootie floundering around in the dark. The curtain jerked halfway open and stuck. Lil's father groaned softly. The audience began to clap, and a moment later they were stomping rhythmically. Then with a mighty jerk the curtain opened all the way. So much for Tootie Gallagher's wonderful brother, Lil thought with satisfaction.

The stage was dark, but suddenly the lights blazed and the audience applauded the brightly painted backdrop of a New York skyline. To an offstage piano, played loudly and enthusiastically by the organist from the Catholic church, the Mothers' Club Follies chorus line, arms around one another, one-stepped onto the stage dressed in elaborate turn-of-the-century costumes: long, full skirts, ruffled blouses with leg-o'-mutton sleeves, huge hats, and parasols. The audience roared approval. The chorus was singing "Good-bye Broadway, Hello France," and at the end they unfurled tiny American flags.

Lil's mother was not in the chorus. Directing the show, she said, was agony enough. And she would be doing a recitation. Jay's mother was there, though, and Tootie's, and Lil's Sunday-school teacher, and several of the women from her mother's knitting circle.

She turned around to see how Jay was taking it. He was slumped in his seat, his hand to his face, peeking over the tops of his fingers and trying to look as if he were not there.

Lil's Sunday-school teacher tripped over her neighbor's feet as they pranced offstage. People laughed and applauded, and Lil wondered if the woman would ever be able to read the Sunday lesson again without giggles from the class.

Mrs. Kelly, the druggist's plump wife, came out and sang "Will You Remember, Sweetheart?"

"Not a dry eye in the house," Lil's father muttered during the applause.

Lil glanced at him to see if he was laughing at the Mothers' Club, but he had a perfectly straight face. You couldn't always tell by that, though.

Mrs. Kelly sang an encore, "Smiles," and some people in the audience sang along.

Two women whom Lil didn't know came out in ragged

overalls and caps and told jokes. They weren't very good jokes, and Lil had read most of them in the *Boston Herald* funnies page. But everybody laughed as if they were the funniest jokes ever told.

Lil was getting restless. It was hard to sit still for so long on those wooden seats. She clapped dutifully for Tootie's mother's interpretative dance, and for the harmonizing of the Mothers' Beauty Shop Quartet, and another chorus number in which the women were dressed like babies in huge bonnets and rompers. They sang "They Go Wild, Simply Wild Over Me," which seemed to Lil not exactly appropriate. At the end they exited waving large rattles.

During the intermission Lil joined Jay and Tootie in the hall. They scurried upstairs and examined the brass nameplates on the offices of the town clerk, the selectmen, the town treasurer.

"I'm going to be chairman of selectmen when I grow up," Jay said. "And I'm going to get this town a merry-go-round. Year-round."

"And slides," Tootie said. "I'll vote for you, Jay. How did you like my mother's dance, Lil?"

"Fine," Lil said vaguely.

"I think the whole thing stinks," Jay said.

"Are you saying my mother stinks?" Tootie balled up her fist. "My mother won't let me say 'stink,' " she added virtuously.

"You just did. Anyway, I mean all of 'em. Pretending to be babies. It's sickening."

Lil agreed with Jay, although she couldn't say so. "I'm never going to join the Mothers' Club," she said.

"I am," Tootie said. "I may be president."

They wandered back to their seats. Lil was getting nervous. She didn't know what her mother's act was going to be, but she knew it was more ambitious than anything she usually did. She had spent a lot of time practicing in her bedroom with the door closed. What if she forgot her lines? What if she wasn't any good at it anymore? Lil's stomach hurt. Everybody was laughing at Mrs. Mattie Spivak's clown act, even when she juggled some balls and dropped them all. In fact that was when they laughed the hardest. Lil couldn't keep her mind on Mrs. Spivak.

She felt sicker and sicker as the other acts went by. Her mother's was last. Then there she was, looking beautiful in a long silver sheath with her hair piled on top of her head. Lil heard her father give a little gasp. The audience quieted as she stood there, poised and waiting.

Lil had never thought a whole lot about how beautiful her mother's voice was until now. She held her breath as her mother said, "I am going to recite two poems by young Englishmen who fought bravely for us." She paused, and there was not a sound in the hall. "The first one is by Wilfrid Wilson Gibson, and it is called 'A Lament.' " She paused again and folded her hands loosely and gazed over the heads of the audience as if she were seeing some far-off battlefield.

She began, her voice low and resonant.

> We who are left, how shall we look again
> Happily on the sun, or feel the rain,
> Without remembering how they who went
> Ungrudgingly, and spent
> Their all for us, loved, too, the sun and rain?

Lil hardly heard the second verse because the poem made her think of Ernie, and she was fighting tears. It would be humiliating to cry in public. She knew from the sound of Mary's breathing that she was moved, too, but she didn't dare look at her.

At the end of the poem there was no sound except a kind of collective sigh.

"The second poem is by Rupert Brooke, and it is called 'The Soldier.' "

> If I should die, think only this of me:
>   That there's some corner of a foreign field
> That is for ever England. There shall be
>   In that rich earth a richer dust concealed;

A dust whom England bore, shaped, made aware,
  Gave, once, her flowers to love, her ways to roam,
A body of England's, breathing English air,
  Washed by the rivers, blest by suns of home.

Lil could hardly hear the words of the second verse because she was imagining Ernie riding his motorcycle in the wind and the rain, bringing wildflowers to Mary, being happy. Tears streamed down her face as her mother finished the last verse:

In hearts at peace, under an English heaven.

The only sound in the hall was the quiet sobbing of a woman in the back. Then a storm of applause broke, and people were on their feet. Lil stood up, mopping her face with her father's handkerchief and holding tight to his hand. Her mother stood there smiling and bowing, and she kept thinking, Is that really my mother? I never knew her. It was both a frightening and a thrilling thought. Her mother really was an actress; she could make people cry. She could make her own daughter cry. Lil stared and stared at her, trying to make her familiar. My mother is a star, she said to herself.

When the audience finally quieted down, Lil's mother said in that quiet but carrying voice, "Two years ago, in a far-off land, the soldier Rupert Brooke died. He rests now in some corner of a foreign field." She inclined her head slightly and walked offstage, again to that stunning silence.

Before it could be broken, Mr. Mel Wheeler bustled onstage to do his four-minute-man talk. It was pretty much the same razzle-dazzle; support our boys, buy bonds, knit, the same talk he gave over and over, wherever a group of people gathered in a public place. Lil had been moved by it before, but now she wished he would be quiet so she could keep the glow her mother's recitation had given her.

Then there were curtain calls for everybody and a long ovation for Lil's mother, who stood there smiling and smiling and bowing, just like the real Lillian Gish.

As Lil and Mary and Lil's father made their way through the crowd, Janice Ward reached out and caught Lil's arm. Janice looked shiny-eyed, as if she had shed tears, and she was clinging to the arm of her lieutenant, who looked self-conscious and proud of himself.

"Oh, Lillian," Janice said, "your mother was wonderful."

Janice Ward had never spoken to her that way before. Lil was awed.

Her father winked at her as they went outside. He, too, had been stopped and congratulated many times.

"Reflected glory," he said to Lil.

She leaned against him. "Golly," she said.

He squeezed her hand. "Double golly. Let's see if we can find the auto in all this mob."

It was a moonlit night, and the stars looked unusually close. Lil looked up at the sky. Ernie, she thought, you would have loved it. She wished she could show her mother how proud she was. Maybe tomorrow she would wear a hair ribbon.

Chapter
TEN

◻◦◻◦◻◦◻◦◻◦◻◦◻◦◻

PEOPLE TALKED ABOUT Lil's mother and the Mothers' Club show for a day or two, but then there were other things to talk about. The Kelleher boy, whose family were patients of her father, was killed when the section of trench he was in was hit by a German shell. The Catholic church had a memorial service for him, and the younger Kellehers stayed home from school for several days. Everyone was nice to them, and for a few weeks people who had bought kerosene and coal oil from the Leonards switched to the Kelleher brothers.

Lil offered to wear one of the hated hair ribbons to

school the day they dedicated the new flag to Michael Kelleher, but her father told her it was a nice thought but she was too old for hair ribbons. She could have kissed him, but since it was a solemn occasion, she confined herself to a sedate thank-you.

Later she gave a whoop of pleasure as she told Jay about it. But Jay wasn't interested in hair ribbons; his father had sent him a wireless set, and he spent all his free time learning the Morse code. Since it was no fun sending messages to himself, he enlisted Lil as his aide.

"I tried to teach Charlie," Jay said, "but he's got a block of cement for a head. He couldn't even remember the S.O.S."

Lil took to it immediately, and after a few afternoons of practice, they settled down in earnest to their wireless sessions in Jay's basement. Sometimes they sent personal messages to each other, from their tables at opposite ends of the basement, but mostly they stayed with serious-sounding war news. Both of them read the daily papers to get the latest war news, but Lil was the most thorough. She never stopped at headlines.

She would send him messages about what was actually happening on the Front, as if from one commanding officer to another. For instance: *Germans take three hundred thousand troops in Italy, followed by stalemate.* Jay would acknowledge receipt of message and ask for details. She would give him as many as she had and make up a few more. But the rule was that the big headline news had to be true, or at least true according to the papers.

Between the bike and the wireless, she had neglected Danny Moe. She felt bad when she realized that she had forgotten to meet him at the Home Guard drill for the second time. She thought of it when she saw him in school the morning after, and he gave her a hurt look. She felt so bad about it that she made up a story about having to go somewhere with her mother. It was obvious, though, that Danny didn't believe her, and that made her feel even worse. Her mother had told her more than once that she was a poor liar. "It shows all over your face when you're lying," she had said. Lil had worked hard to develop a poker face so that nobody would ever know how she was feeling, but it hadn't worked. So she just reminded Danny of the Halloween party and hoped that would make up for her neglect.

The day before Halloween on her way home from school she passed the shoemaker's shop. There was a Closed sign in the window. Probably Fancy Pantsy was off spying somewhere.

When she got home, her mother was not there. It was knitting circle day. Mary was not around either. Lil's father had told her to leave Mary alone when she was having one of her bad days. That meant when she was feeling bad about Ernie.

Lil changed into an old khaki skirt and her favorite sweater, which she was not supposed to wear to play in, but her mother wasn't home to object. It was a dark red cashmere sweater that her grandmother had sent her. Then, before she went out, she put on the white navy cap that Ernie had left her. She didn't wear it outside very much, because she was afraid she would lose it, but today she needed to feel close to Ernie. Sometimes he seemed so far away.

Jay and Charlie and Tootie came by. She didn't want to go with Tootie and Charlie, but she didn't want to stay home alone, either, so she joined them.

They walked along the river, over bumpy ground. The brilliant autumn leaves still clung to the trees but one good rain would send them fluttering to the ground. Lil loved winter, but her father hated it. When snow came, he had to put up his auto and hire a sleigh at the livery stable. He suffered from chilblains, and sometimes he ran up and down the yard in the snow in his bare feet, because that was supposed to help cure it.

"So where are we going?" Jay said finally as they all stopped and flung themselves in the grass to rest.

"Let's go climb the Essex train," Tootie said.

"We've done that a thousand times." The one car that brought commuters from Essex every morning to connect with the train to Boston sat on the tracks all day, about a quarter of a mile behind Lil's house. At night the engine returned, and the commuters were taken back to Essex. When she had first come to town, she had been enthralled with the train, but she had explored it very thoroughly many times, and it no longer held any interest for her.

"We could attack it," Jay said, lifting his finger and aiming it as if it were a gun. "We can charge the German lines and capture the train."

"Great!" Charlie liked anything to do with war. "Let's go." He pedaled off at high speed.

"Last one there is a rotten egg," Tootie said, and whooshed past Lil.

Lil considered going home. She did not want to pretend to be charging a German train. It was childish. Besides, Charlie and Tootie could get rough when they thought they had an excuse for it. But the thought of going home to the silent house did not appeal to her. She sighed and followed the others.

Maybe if she could get their minds off the silly train, they could make plans for tomorrow night. Her mother had been talking for days about the little party before the kids went out to spook people. She had persuaded Lil to give up on the dinosaur costume idea because nobody seemed to know how to make it, but she had brought a wonderful skull mask from Denison's, and she was cutting up a shaggy white fur coat to fit Lil.

Lil had tried it on yesterday and scared Mary half to death. The coat came almost to her ankles, and the sleeves were long enough to hide her hands. Her mother had cut off part of the coat to make a long, shaggy wig. Lil looked like some kind of weird monster.

Thinking about the costume, she cheered up and pumped her bike so hard, she almost caught up with the others. They were throwing their bikes down beside the barbed-wire fence that bordered the railroad tracks. Lil laid hers down carefully. She didn't want to scratch the pretty blue paint or get any dents.

Clutching her sailor hat, she followed the others through the barbed-wire fence. Jay held the strands apart for her, which surprised her. You never knew about Jay.

They lay in the long grass and "studied the situation." Then Jay, who had appointed himself commander of the unit, gave instructions in a low voice. They would charge when he gave the signal, storming the train from different angles, firing their weapons repeatedly.

"We've got 'em outnumbered," Jay said. He was always so serious and intense about war games, it almost made them seem real. Lil had to remind herself that it was just a silly kids' game.

He began to count, slowly, and in spite of herself Lil felt tense.

". . . six, seven, eight, nine, ten—*charge!*"

As they broke out of the grass, Lil tripped and nearly fell flat. She had been assigned to the caboose end. The air was full of shouted *bangs!* and as she clambered up the iron ladder, the others had disappeared. For a crazy moment she was really scared. She knew there wasn't a soul on the train, let alone a German. But what if . . . ? She threw open the door into the car almost frantically, pushing with all her strength. It opened more easily than she expected, and she fell against the dusty plush of the end seat.

Jay was prancing down the aisle. "Say 'Kamerad,' you filthy Hun!"

He wasn't getting it right. She had told him before, "kamerad" meant comrade. But Jay had it fixed in his mind that it meant "I give up."

Charlie crawled down from the top of the car and came in feetfirst. Tootie was crouched at the other end, snarling ferociously.

Lil sat down. "All right, they're all dead. What do we do now?"

It was always the same: The noble side won, the enemy was dead, and then what? They looked at each other blankly.

"Let's go look for apples on the ground that haven't got worms in them," Lil said.

"Why don't you tell about your party?" Tootie said.

"We're going to have Wart Cake and Bat's Wings,

Demon's Draught, and Sand Witches," Lil said.

"You're making it up," Tootie said.

"I am not. My mother got the recipes from a book. And wait till you see my costume. You'll faint."

"That'll be the day, when you make me faint," Tootie said.

"What are we going to do after the party?" Lil said, changing the subject. Tootie, she thought, was in for a surprise.

"The usual," said Jay. "Soap windows, scare people. What we've been talking about."

"We could scare Fancy Pantsy," Lil suggested. "We could write *spy* on his door, so everyone would know." That was something she'd been thinking about.

"Not bad," said Tootie. "Come on, let's go."

They all trooped off the train and across the field. But at least, Lil thought, she'd had one idea Tootie hadn't put down.

Lil got caught in the barbed wire, and Jay held it up for her.

"Oh, blah, here comes Hot Dog," Charlie said.

"He can be the enemy," Jay said. "He doesn't mind."

"Hey, Hot Dog." The boys and Tootie greeted Hot Dog with such enthusiasm that he looked bewildered.

"Don't hurt him," Lillian said. She liked Hot Dog. He wasn't like Fancy Pantsy, a spy who deserved what he got.

"Who's going to hurt him?" Jay said. "Hey, Hot Dog, you want to play Germans and Yanks?"

Hot Dog's big, placid face broke into a slow smile. "Yeah. That'd be fun."

"You can be the German, and we'll be the Yanks."

"Not me," Lillian said. She was afraid they'd scare Hot Dog.

"All right, you can be the foreign correspondent," Jay said. "You can file the story." He took off his belt.

"If you hit him, I'll tell!" Lil said.

Jay gave her a withering look. "How dumb can you be! We aren't going to hit anybody. Hot Dog, back up to that fence post, all right?"

Obediently Hot Dog backed up to the post and waited.

Lil thought of the statement that Mr. Barnum of the circus was supposed to have said: "There's one born every minute." She felt embarrassed for Hot Dog, but she didn't know how to change what was happening.

Jay efficiently strapped Hot Dog's wrists behind the post. "Don't move now, or you'll get caught in the wire."

"Some war," Lil said. "Three to one, and the enemy all tied up."

"Be quiet," Jay said, "or I'll take away your correspondent's pass."

"Lil is a big coward," Tootie said. "She ought to have a yellow flag tied to her."

"You shut up," Lil said.

Tootie started toward her, holding a stick she had picked up in a threatening way, but Jay grabbed her arm.

"Where's your discipline?" he snapped. "All troops, lie down. Prone position, facing the enemy. Take aim." He gave Tootie a shove, and Lil giggled.

The three of them lay on their stomachs in the long grass, aiming sticks at Hot Dog, who was beginning to look nervous.

"Ready . . . aim . . . fire!" Jay's stern voice called out the commands. At the word "fire," they all began yelling "Ack ack ack ack" very loud and fast.

Hot Dog flinched and tried to pull loose.

"Company . . . move up!"

The troops squirmed forward.

"Company . . . aim . . . fire!"

Lil heard Hot Dog say, "Can we stop now?" but no one paid any attention to him.

"Cut it out," Lil said. "Let him loose." But they ignored her, too.

Tootie's eyes glowed with the spirit of battle. "Attack!" she yelled. "Attack!"

Hot Dog began to whimper.

Jay yelled, "Hold it! I'm commander here."

But neither Tootie nor Charlie paid any attention to him.

"Attack . . . charge!" Tootie screamed, and she and

Charlie rose up from the grass and dove at Hot Dog with their sticks.

He screamed and tried to pull loose from the fence, but every time he moved, the barbed wire jabbed him. He began to cry.

Tootie had her stick shoved against his stomach, and Charlie was crowding her, waiting for his turn. Lil couldn't stand it. She leaped toward Tootie and pulled her away from Hot Dog. Tootie turned on her furiously and shoved her hard into the fence. Lil yelped as she felt the barbs dig into her back. She tried to get her balance, but the sleeve of her sweater caught.

"Retreat!" Jay was yelling. "Let her alone." Roughly he shoved Charlie out of the way and tried to grab Tootie. She dodged out of his reach and yanked the sailor cap off Lil's head. As she ran with it, Charlie followed her. Jay hesitated a moment.

Lil was yelling, "Give me back my navy hat! I'll kill you, Tootie Gallagher! My hat!"

Hot Dog was moaning, and huge tears rolled down his cheeks.

Jay fled.

"The skunks," Lil said. "Stop crying, Hot Dog. We've got to get out of this."

Hot Dog's lip trembled, but he made a mighty effort to stop crying. "I thought they just wanted to play," he said in a quavery voice. "They were mean." He tried again to get his hands loose.

"Hold still. You'll just get hung up worse." She leaned away from the fence cautiously and felt her favorite sweater tear in the shoulder. "Damn!" she said.

Hot Dog said, "You swore."

"Damn, damn, damn. It's my best sweater. My mother will kill me. I'll kill *myself*. My *best* sweater." She got her sleeve loose, but there was a ragged scratch on her arm.

She let herself carefully through the fence and struggled with the belt that held Hot Dog's wrists. It was so tight, it was a wonder his blood could circulate. "If Tootie loses my navy hat, I'll . . ."

"You'll kill her," Hot Dog said.

"I will."

He twisted his head around to look at her. "Will you really?"

"Of course not. But I'll do something terrible."

"Ouch," Hot Dog said as she pulled at the strap.

She looked up as somebody yelled, "Hey." It was Jay running toward them. Lil held up her fists. "You go away. Get out of here."

"Hold your horses," he said. He ran up to her and handed her her navy hat. Then he let himself through the fence and undid the strap. "You're loose, Hot Dog."

Hot Dog stepped away from the fence and rubbed his wrists. "I thought you were the enemy," he said.

"So did I," Lil said. She glared at Jay. But at least she had her hat back. She jammed it on her head.

"They mutinied," he said. "They disobeyed orders."

"I'm going home," Hot Dog said. He lumbered off across the field.

"You're bleeding," Jay said to Lil.

"I tore my best sweater."

He looked at it, chewing his lip. "You didn't get a heart attack or anything, did you?"

"I don't get heart attacks. Hold the fence while I crawl through."

"Yes, you do. My mother said so." He held the strands of wire apart while she wriggled through, and then she held them for him.

"My mother is going to kill me when she sees this sweater."

"You could hide it."

"My mother has X-ray eyes."

Jay trotted along beside her in silence for a minute. "That Tootie gets too wild sometimes."

"She's a monster."

"Charlie *seems* wild, but it's more that he hasn't got good sense." Jay stopped and retied his bootlace, but Lil didn't wait for him. He ran to catch up. "It's going to be a swell party tomorrow, huh?"

"A beaut."

"One thing I'll say for our mothers—when they throw a party, they throw a dilly."

It was rather pleasant to have Jay in such an agreeable frame of mind. She knew he was scared she'd tell on him about how mean they were to Hot Dog. Well, of course she wouldn't tell, but on the other hand she'd let Jay stew about it for a while, wondering whether she would or not.

"I don't feel like having Tootie and Charlie to the party now."

"We have to," Jay said. "Our mothers already asked their mothers if they could come. Besides, we didn't invite anybody else."

"I invited Danny Moe."

Jay looked surprised. "Is he coming?"

"I guess so."

"He's just a baby."

"He's in our room."

"Only because he skipped a grade."

"Well, so did I. Anyway, I asked him. I like him."

"He's all right. You got any nifty ideas for haunting people, besides painting Fancy Pantsy's door?"

"I'm working on it."

"We could paint Miss Emerson's fence bright red."

"No, it would take too long." The idea of vandalizing an old lady didn't appeal to Lillian. "We could turn your dog green. I know how."

"Oh, don't be a dope. You'd have to paint him, and my mother would kill me."

"No, it'll come off in an ordinary bath."

"You're crazy."

She smiled smugly. "I know how to do it."

"I don't believe you, but anyway forget it."

"Bring him over to my house tomorrow after school, and I'll prove it." She jumped up the steps onto her back porch.

He stood looking at her. "You aren't going to tell, are you?"

Lil wagged her head. "I'll see." She went into the house.

"Glory be to God, what's happened to you now?" Mary said. "You look like a Halloween witch yourself. What did you do to your best sweater? Your mother will have your scalp."

"You don't have to tell her, do you? It was an accident."

"Take it off and let me have a look." She took the sweater from Lil. "I might be able to stitch it together so it won't show, but it won't hold up."

"I'll hide it. Is there anything to eat?"

"Two molasses cookies and a glass of milk. Supper

is only an hour away. And I've got crazy things to make for tomorrow, accordin' to your mother's orders. Bat's Wings, indeed! 'Tis only molasses cookies with green colorin'. Demon's Draught, sweet cider, that's all. But maybe you'll be tellin' me how I make Wart Cake out of sponge cake with raisins. Whoever heard of raisins in my good sponge cake? It's heathen, that's what it is."

"I think I'll tell Tootie Gallagher she can't come to my party," Lil said.

"You're too late, darlin'. Her mother is sending round a batch of cookies for you witches and goblins. Frosted with arsenic, probably."

On her way upstairs, Lil thought it might be a pretty good party just the same, if she could keep herself from punching Tootie Gallagher in the stomach.

Chapter
ELEVEN

☐!☐!☐!☐!☐!☐!☐!☐

IT WAS HALLOWEEN at last. School was abuzz with anticipation. Pumpkins with grinning faces sat on the windowsills, and in the younger grades the children had drawn enormous pictures of monsters and witches and ghosts. The principal called a special assembly, and they all sang a song called "Halloween Frolic," which began "A little witch in a steeple hat/Once tried a merry spell." But Lil was disappointed in the merry spell. It was just a few magic words that called all the rabbits out of the woods. Who was scared of rabbits?

She liked better the poem that Miss Smith from the office recited, wearing a pointed black cap and an orange necktie with witches on it. She said the poem was by Oliver Wendell Holmes, and she read it in a scary way:

Look out, look out, boys, clear the track!
The witches are here! They've all come back!
· · · · · · · · · · · ·
On their well-trained broomsticks mounted high
Seen like shadows against the sky;
Crossing the tracks of owls and bats,
Hugging before them their coal-black cats.

Miss Smith was the one who had shown Lil where the fourth grade was, on that first day of school long ago. Lil had grown to like her quite a lot. She usually had something funny to say. Her reading of the poem brought a lot of applause.

School let out half an hour early, and Lil was glad, because she had a lot to do. First she went to the fruit store to buy a pound of capers, but the only capers available were in tiny bottles and rather expensive. She tried to think what to do. She had promised to turn Jay's dog green, and she had to come up with something. She decided to buy some spinach and try that. It turned the cooking water green, too; she knew that.

When she had changed her clothes, she rode her bike to Jay's house. Luckily his mother was at her house and there was no one around except the housekeeper, who didn't care what they did as long as they didn't mess up her kitchen. She gave them each a glass of milk and some molasses hermits and left them.

Jay went out to the run where the dog spent most of his time. The dog's name was Archie, although it had a much longer and fancier kennel name. Archie was a purebred standard poodle, and he was really not Jay's dog at all but his mother's. She was very proud of him and took him to Boston to AKC dog shows.

"It won't hurt him, will it?" Jay said as he came into the kitchen, leaning backward against Archie's pull on the leash.

Archie put his paws on Lil's chest and kissed her face in big, slurpy swipes of his tongue.

"Archie, cut it out." She pushed him away as she dumped the spinach into one of Mrs. Collier's copper kettles and began pouring water on it. "Get the fire going good," she told Jay.

He got the coal shovel and filled it with coal from the shiny copper coal hod that stood by the stove. "It's pretty hot anyway. Mrs. Baxter's been making soup." He helped Lil lift the heavy kettle onto the shiny black iron stove.

"Now we have to wait," she said.

"How long?"

"I don't know. Till it distills."

"What's 'distilled'?"

Lil waved her hand airily. "Oh, steams and all."

"Then it ought to have a cover on it. It won't steam without a cover."

It always irked Lil that Jay knew more about things like that than she did. He even knew how to make cinnamon toast.

"I was just going to put a cover on," she said. She found one that more or less fitted the kettle.

"Let's go play wireless while it distills," Jay said.

They went down into the basement, where Jay had fitted up his wireless operator's room. At each end of the long room a small table was set up with a receiving and sending set. One end was Brigadier General Jay Collier's headquarters, and the other end was Lieutenant General Lillian G. Adams's quarters. They had quite a lot of argument about rank until Lil hit on the idea of both of them being generals. She was not sure whether a brigadier or a lieutenant general was the higher rank, but she had decided not to press the point. General Collier was behind the lines in Operations, and General Adams was up near the Front, directing the action.

At first Archie disrupted their communications by leaping on them and racing around, but finally he found an old overshoe and settled down to chew on it.

Lil had overslept that morning and had not had a chance to read the headlines, but they had a message to cover that situation. *HQ HQ HQ*, she tapped out with brisk efficiency, *Gen Adams to Gen Collier All quiet on this front. Acknowledge.*

Jay was now free to improvise. She watched his bent head at the other end of the long table as he thought about what to send. For a crazy moment she thought, "What if this were real?" The day before yesterday had been Ernie's eighteenth birthday, and although they had all tried to act cheerful, it hadn't been easy. It was a long time since they had had any word of him, and the news was full of ships lost at sea. What if Jay were about to send her a message that Ernie's ship was sunk? Panic clutched at her stomach, and she wanted to call to him not to send a message.

But here it came, and she switched her set to receiving. *Front lines. Collier to Adams. All quiet here too. We are ready for anything. Repeat we are ready. Over.*

She was trying to think of some questions about troop strength, but suddenly Jay looked up and said, "I smell something funny."

"The spinach!"

They clattered upstairs to the kitchen. The water in

the kettle had boiled away, and the spinach was a dark green blob stuck to the bottom.

"That's all right," Lillian said. "It saves us having to pour out the first bunch of water." She added water from the teakettle to the mass of spinach. "It has to distill twice. We'd better stay here and watch."

"It won't turn him green permanent, will it? Get down, Archie." He pushed at the dog's snowy white ruff. "Maybe it's not such a hot idea. My mother will be wild if she sees him green. There's a dog show in Topsfield next week."

"It'll wash out," Lil said, although she didn't know whether it would or not. Danny hadn't said.

They had another molasses hermit.

"These are almost as good as Mary's," Lil said. "You ought to see the stuff Mary's cooking for the party." She looked at the clock. "I have to be home in half an hour. Is your costume ready?"

"Sure. If you tell me what yours is, I'll tell you mine."

"Nope. I want to surprise everybody."

"I got a little can of green paint at the dime store."

"What for?"

"To paint stuff on Mr. Panzi's door. Charlie and Tootie both think it's a swell idea."

Lil had forgotten all about her suggestion. "Maybe we better not do it. Paint won't come off. We might get arrested." Lil had had a brief lecture from her father that morning about the difference between fun and destruction.

"Ah, the only policeman is Ray Wilson, and he can't watch everybody at once. We can dodge him easy."

Lil shrugged. She was not one to back down, especially on an idea of her own that had been accepted as brilliant. "The spinach is boiling." She lifted the lid and got a faceful of hot steam. "It looks green enough." She pushed the heavy kettle over to the cold part of the stove. "Now we pour out the water and wash Archie."

"What do we do with the spinach?" Jay peered over her shoulder. "Yuck! It looks disgusting."

"Spinach is always disgusting." She leaned closer to the kettle. "There isn't very much liquid left. I hope it's enough. Have you got a little bowl or a dipper or something we can pour it into?" As Archie sniffed inquisitively, she said, "Lucky old you, Archie. You're going to turn bright green for Halloween. Boy, is your owner going to be surprised."

"Is she ever," Jay muttered. He was plainly beginning to have doubts. But he brought a small tin dipper and together they lifted the heavy kettle off the stove and poured the dark green juice into it.

As they were draining out the last drops of spinach juice, Archie danced around them and pushed against

Jay with his front paws.

"Watch it!" Jay yelled.

But it was too late. The kettle and the dipper crashed to the kitchen floor. A large, wet blob of spinach plopped onto Archie's white coat and fell off onto the floor, and the juice trickled slowly and sickeningly toward the kitchen table.

Jay collapsed on the floor in a heap. "They'll murder me," he moaned. "They'll boil me in oil."

Lil swallowed hard. Then she pulled herself together and said briskly, "Well, don't just sit there. Get the mop."

Jay got to his feet, looking thoroughly discouraged. "You and your green dogs." He brought a small garbage can from under the sink.

Lil looked into it. "It looks so clean. Don't you people ever have any garbage?" She had learned a long time ago that when something bad happened that she could be blamed for, it was a good idea to find something that would make the other person feel guilty. Even if it was only an unnaturally clean garbage pail.

Jay rose to the bait. "We *wash* our garbage pails once in a while," he snarled. "Where's that darned mop?" He was rummaging through the broom closet, throwing aside brooms and carpet sweeper and dust cloths.

Lil gingerly lifted some of the hot spinach and let it

fall into the pail with a dull thud. She looked at the juice trickling down her arms. "He would have turned a beautiful green."

Mrs. Baxter burst into the kitchen like a whole coven of witches. "What's going on here? What's all that noise? Oh, my saints above, look at my clean kitchen!" Her voice rose in a wail.

Lil backed away. "We'll clean it up, Mrs. Baxter. It was an accident."

"Accident! Jay, get out of that closet! What are you . . ." She found herself stepping in a puddle of spinach juice. "Oh, it's too much! Get out of here, git!" She flapped her apron at them. "Right now, before I lose what wits I got left."

"We'll clean up . . ." Jay began.

"You'll clean nothing. Just let me see the backs of your heels. Go on, beat it. Oh, I could cry."

"Don't cry, Mrs. Baxter," Lil said. "We're sorry."

"Sorry is as sorry does." She shooed them toward the door. "Out!"

When they were out in the backyard, Lil said, "Whew! What a temper."

"If she tells my mother, I probably won't get to your party," Jay said. "I might not even get to go out at all."

Lil tried to sound hopeful. "She won't tell. Anyway

your mother is helping my mother with the party. She won't want to miss it. They like parties better than we do. All that crepe paper and stuff."

"Maybe if I carry up a hodful of coal for her, Mrs. Baxter will feel better. She doesn't like to do that."

"All right. Carry two hods. I have to go." Lil got on her bike and took off for home. It was too bad they couldn't have dyed Archie green. He would have looked spectacular.

Chapter
TWELVE

0:0:0:0:0:0:0:0

LIL'S MOTHER and Jay's mother were in the dining room, setting the Halloween table. They had festooned orange and black crepe paper from the chandelier to the corners of the room. There was a big pumpkin in the center of the table, and small tin ones in front of each plate. A huge black paper witch was stuck to the wall over the sideboard. Mrs. Collier was sticking tiny orange candles in individual pumpkins at each place.

"Just pray they don't set the house on fire," she said. "Hi, Lil. How do you like it?"

"Great," Lil said. "It looks wonderful. There are supposed to be five places, though. You've only got four."

Her mother stopped in the midst of putting Halloween paper napkins at every place. "I thought there were four. You, Jay, Tootie, and Charlie."

"And Danny. I invited Danny."

"Who is Danny?"

"Oh, you know, Mother. Danny Moe. He lives up at the Grove."

"Do I know his mother?"

"He hasn't got one. She's dead."

Her mother looked at Mrs. Collier. "Moe?"

Lil tensed. She was afraid Mrs. Collier would say, "You mean that Socialist."

But she just shook her head. "I don't know the Grove people."

"Well, if you've invited him, you've invited him, but I wish you'd told me. Do we have enough favors, Bess?"

"I think there are six of everything in those packages."

"I told the mothers to have the children bring their costumes so they can dress up after they eat. Otherwise it will be a mess. Will that Grove boy come in his costume?"

"I don't know." Lil decided to get out of the way before her mother thought of any more problems. She went into her father's office.

He was pouring some tablets out of a bottle into one of the small envelopes in which he dispensed medicine. He finished counting the tablets and put the big bottle back on the shelf among the rows and rows of medicine. "Hi."

"Hi," Lil said. She settled down in one of the two oak chairs that patients sat in. "Who's sick?"

He made a face. "Who isn't? These are for the Bennett boy. He's got German measles. I hope we don't get an epidemic of that."

She frowned. "Mrs. Mason says we should call it Liberty measles."

He laughed. "I'll tell that to Andy Bennett, so he can enjoy it." He sat down in front of his big rolltop desk and swiveled his chair around to look at her. "I suppose you've got outrageous plans for tonight."

"Pretty outrageous."

The phone rang, and while he asked the person on the other end the familiar questions—"Has she got a fever? . . . Does her head ache? . . . How's her appetite?"—Lil leafed through one of his medical magazines, looking at the pictures of somebody's pancreas and somebody else's skeleton. The skeleton reminded her that she'd better go check on her costume. It was going to be a dandy. She got up and started out.

"Lil . . ." Her father had hung up the phone and

was putting on his suit coat. "Don't get into trouble tonight."

"I won't."

He reached for his hat. "And take it easy with Mr. Panzi. I know he's one of the favorite targets, but lay off, will you?"

"Why?"

"Well, he's had trouble enough in his life."

She followed him to the door. "Daddy, is he a German?"

"No, he is not. He came many years ago from Kiev, in Russia. All his family except his grandfather were killed in a pogrom. I have to run." He kissed her cheek and left.

She went upstairs trying to make sense out of what he had said. According to the papers, Russians were bad people, too. There was that revolution, and all those Communists. Whatever a Communist was. But if Mr. Panzi had come here years ago, maybe he wasn't a Communist or a Bolshevik or anything like that. It sort of spoiled the fun to think of Mr. Panzi not being a spy. Of course he still *could* be. Anybody that mean was bound to be something. She wondered what a pogrom was.

She got her costume out of the closet and put it on. She wasn't sure what kind of fur it was. It was long and shaggy and white. The wig that her mother had made hung to her shoulders when she put it on. But then she had to take it off again to put the skull mask on. When everything was in place, she looked in her full-length mirror. Her heart jumped. She scared herself. The sleeves of the coat were almost as long as the coat itself. She flapped her arms at her mirror image and said, "Yah! Yah!" The result was really horrible. The skull had big eye sockets, with eyebrows penciled in. There was a triangular hole where her nose was, and a wide grin showing huge rows of teeth. The fur on the wig stood up on top, as if she were some hairy animal that had been out in a strong wind. Oh, she would give people heart attacks tonight, all right. She had to give her mother credit, she was a whiz-bang costume maker.

She took off the costume and put on the dress her mother had laid out for her to wear at the supper. The dress was pretty boring after that costume, but the supper wouldn't last long. The kids were coming at five, and as soon as they'd eaten, they could go out.

She went downstairs when she heard the doorbell ring. It was Jay, giving sidewise glances at his mother to see if she had heard about the spinach. Both mothers were in a good mood, and Jay shot Lil a glance of relief. If Mrs. Baxter told after Halloween was over, it wouldn't be such a disaster.

Tootie came next, looking unusually clean and tidy. Lil didn't want to speak to her, but she knew her mother would be mad if she didn't.

"Take Tootie upstairs, dear," her mother said, "so she can leave her costume in your room. Jay, you can put yours in the spare room."

"You haven't said what you're going to wear," Tootie said, putting her small suitcase on Lil's bed.

"And I'm not going to," Lil said, leaving the room. She knew she was being rude, but it would be even ruder if she punched Tootie in the stomach, which was what she longed to do. She was worried about Hot Dog. He hadn't come to school all day. Maybe he'd really gotten hurt. She had thought about going to see him, but she didn't know where he lived.

"Hot Dog wasn't in school," she said accusingly, when Tootie came downstairs.

"What of it? He's so dumb, he doesn't come to school half the time anyway."

Lil clenched her teeth and said under her breath, "I ought to beat you up."

"Try it," Tootie said.

At that moment Charlie arrived, clutching his costume under his arm. And a few minutes later Mrs. Collier said, "We'll be ready to eat in a few minutes. Are you sure your other friend is coming, Lillian?"

"Yes," Lil said. He might not, though. Danny was shy. He might be scared to come.

A few minutes later Mary called Lil into the kitchen. "There's a little ghost hanging around the back door," she said. "Anybody you know?"

Lil ran outside. A small figure in a sheet hovered near the sidewalk. A cat's face had been drawn on the sheet, with splendid black whiskers sticking out both sides of the face, and arched eyebrows. "Danny?" Lil wasn't sure.

"Hi." Danny's usually small voice sounded muffled.

"What are you doing out here? Come on in. You look great."

He held out a big tin jack-o'-lantern on a long stick. "My daddy got me this. How do you like it?"

"It's wonderful. You can lift it up to people's windows and scare them to death. Does it have a candle?"

"Yeah. I'm not to light it till later. Where's your costume?"

"I forgot to tell you; we aren't supposed to put them on till after supper."

"Oh." He stopped. "Can I still come in?"

Mary showed up behind them on the steps. "Come on in, little ghostie. You can put your uniform in my room. You look verra fearsome indeed."

They heard Danny's hollow giggle. "All right," he

said. He followed Lil into the kitchen.

The supper was a success, in spite of Tootie's sudden attack of shyness in the presence of adults and Charlie's grabby table manners. Mary and Lil's mother and Jay's mother brought in each dish with great ceremony, announcing the name of it: Bat's Wings for Mary's delicious fried chicken; Graveyard Stew Deluxe for the scalloped potatoes; Witches' Shredded Cape for the lettuce. The cider was Demon's Draught, and Charlie asked if it was hard. The molasses cookies with green coloring had undergone a name change to Wart Cakes, and Mary won the day with her sponge cake, which was as it always was, fluffy and light and unspoiled by raisins.

"What's the name of the cake, Mary?" Jay asked her.

Mary held it high, the way she had carried in Lil's birthday cake. "Irish Angel Cake," she said. "To take the curse off the demons."

Lil noticed her mother looking Danny over critically at first, but he was so quiet and well-mannered, Lil could tell that her mother was impressed. She was a great one for good manners.

After supper they could hardly wait to get into their costumes. Tootie turned into a witch, with a long black cape and a tall pointed cap with "sinful signs" painted on it, and a mask with a fearfully long nose and pointed chin. She twirled in front of Lil's full-length mirror, pleased with herself. But when she saw Lil in her costume, she gasped and said, "That's the most horrible Halloween costume I ever saw."

Lil was pleased. It was the first nice thing Tootie had ever said to her. "You're pretty horrible, too," she said generously.

In Lil's parents' bedroom her mother was applying makeup to Jay, who was not wearing a mask. He was the Devil, in a cut-down pair of his father's trousers, a red vest, and one of his father's jackets. A long forked tail hung down in back, and he had combed his hair forward so that it hung to his eyebrows. He had a very tall hat, bought secondhand from the tailor who sold riding clothes. Lil's mother was painting on a slinky black moustache that curled up at the ends, and she had already given him eyebrows that looked like inverted *V*'s, and a pointed goatee. He did not look like Jay at all.

"You're an artist, Ella," Jay's mother said. "I don't recognize my child."

"Do I scare you?" Jay asked.

"Hold still," Lil's mother said.

Charlie came in to watch. He was dressed in a baggy clown suit with a clown mask. Lil thought he looked good but not scary. His pant legs were too long, and he had to keep hitching them up.

Mary came upstairs, keeping Danny behind her. "I've got a fearful ghost here. Part cat, he is, and you know what *that* means." She scooted past them to the overhead light and pulled the chain, plunging the room into darkness.

"Mary!" Lil's mother wailed. "I can't see what I'm doing."

"It'll keep a minute," Mary said. She went back into the hall and pushed Danny into the room ahead of her.

In the dim light that came from the hall, he did look very ghostly. Mary had added a few touches of her own. A black sash around his waist held the sheet so he wouldn't trip on it. She had cut out some ears from black felt and sewn them to the sheet that covered his head, and she had lighted the candle in his jack-o'-lantern.

For a moment they all stared at him. Only his eyes were visible in the slits cut into the face. In the reflected light of the candle, they looked big and brilliant.

"Ooh!" Tootie said softly.

Mrs. Collier burst out laughing and began to clap. "Bravo! You're terrifying, Danny."

Mary pulled the light chain. "There's fearful things abroad tonight, indeed, indeed."

In spite of herself, Lil shivered. Then she said, "Hurry up, Mother. We have to go."

The telephone rang, and Mary went to answer it on

the phone by the doctor's bed. She pulled the phone out from the wall and took the receiver off the hook. "Dr. Adams's residence." She listened a moment and then said, "Yes, she is." She held out the receiver. "It's for you, Mrs. Collier."

Jay's mother looked surprised. Jay shot a look at Lil, and she knew he was afraid it might be Mrs. Baxter telling his mother about the mess in the kitchen.

But Mrs. Collier was saying, "Oh, it's good to hear your voice, Tom!"

Lil's mother herded the children, except Jay, out of the room and closed the door. "It's Jay's daddy," she explained.

"He's an officer," Lil said, "at Fort Devens."

"I know that," Tootie said. "Everybody knows that."

Lil's urge to punch Tootie returned.

The children went downstairs and waited impatiently for Jay. After a long time he came down slowly. Lil's mother looked at his face and went upstairs. Mary watched her go. Then she said to the children, "All right then, come home before eight-thirty, and don't get in trouble." She shooed them out of the house.

As soon as they were outside, Tootie said to Jay, "I bet you forgot the paint."

"Yeah, I did."

"I knew you would. The best idea we ever had, and

you forget it. Well, I brought shoe blacking and a brush. We're all set." She brandished the bottle of blacking. "Wait till old Fancy Pantsy sees what we do to his door!"

Jay was hanging back as the others rushed down the street. Even quiet Danny had caught the Halloween spirit and was hissing and spitting like a real cat.

Lil waited for Jay. "What's the matter with you?"

In spite of the devilish makeup, his face looked bleak. "My dad's getting shipped out. Tomorrow."

"Oh!" Pictures that Lil had seen flooded her mind: mud, barbed-wire fences, soldiers reeling with fatigue, soldiers dying, shells lighting up the sky like fireworks. She wanted to put her arm around Jay, but he would hit her if she did such a thing. "He'll be all right," she said. "He's an officer. Maybe they'll keep him back in headquarters."

"Yeah," Jay said. In a voice that didn't sound like his, he said, "Well, come on, what are we waiting for?" And he ran out ahead of the others. "The battle plan is Walnut Road first. Ready, men, *advance!*"

"Who put you in charge?" the Witch said.

"I did," said the shaggy White Monster, "and if you don't like it, you can lump it."

The Witch shoved the White Monster, and the White Monster shoved harder.

"Come *on*," the Clown said. "The other kids are going to beat us to the best places."

Groups of children were in sight now, carrying lighted jack-o'-lanterns, wearing sheets, grinning horribly in masks of skulls and goblins. A group of older boys wearing only black masks over their eyes were running up and down the road, beating drums and ringing cowbells. The Ford belonging to the town's chief of police, Ray Wilson, moved slowly down the street and stopped near the railroad station. He and his sometime deputy Banty Moore got out and separated.

"Cops," Charlie said. "Cheese it, the cops."

"They aren't even coming this way," Jay said. He was beginning to sound more like himself. "Let's start with Mrs. Halleck."

Up and down the road they went, ringing doorbells. Sometimes people came out to admire their costumes, sometimes they got a "get out of here" reception, sometimes no one came to the door at all.

"It's time for Mr. Popper," Jay said as they came to a low stucco house with a small pond next to it. "He'll chase us. If he catches you, he'll throw you in the pond."

Some of the older boys who were soaping windows had already been at Mr. Popper's. There were big marks on the glass.

"He don't chase the big kids so much," Charlie said.

Lil hung back. She wanted to torment Mr. Popper, but she did not want to get doused in that cold, slimy water. Danny hung back with her.

"You two are yellow," Tootie said. She had her bottle of shoe blacking in her hand. "I'm going to leave Popper-Popper something to cry about." She ran up to the front door, waving the paintbrush.

Jay dashed past her and rang the doorbell. Before Tootie could leave her mark on Mr. Popper's neatly painted door, the man threw the door open and started after them. He must have been waiting right there, Lil thought. She and Danny and Jay got away, but Tootie lost part of her black cambric cape, and Charlie let out a yell as Mr. Popper grabbed him, marched him double-time to the edge of the pond, and shoved him in.

Lil couldn't help laughing when Charlie caught up with them. He was wet only to his knees; the pond was not deep. But he was mad, and the slimy, wet leaf of a pond lily clung to his sleeve. "You rang the bell too quick," he told Jay.

"Yes, you did," Tootie said. "I didn't have time to black up his door."

"He did not," Lil said. "Mr. Popper was right there. He'd have heard us anyway."

They worked the street thoroughly, enjoying most the few people who were bad-tempered enough to chase them or yell at them. Finally they went back up the road to the square and paused to lay a plan of action.

"We can't do anything to the drugstore," Jay said, "after all the candy Mr. Kelly gives us."

"How about the tailor's?" Charlie said.

"No. He sold me this hat at half price."

"You got too many friends," Tootie said. "I'm going to do a job on the paper store."

But the proprietor of the paper store was sitting on his steps, watching the kids mill up and down Railroad Avenue, calling out encouragement to them from time to time, but also making sure his own place didn't get vandalized.

Upstairs in the three-story "Block," a dinner party for adults was going on in the Elks' hall. The children could hear the music. Half a dozen Fords and one Maxwell were parked in front, along with many buggies and carriages. Janice Ward was driving slowly up the street, all alone.

"Let's let the horses loose," Charlie said.

"No," Jay said. He had been almost run over by a runaway horse once, and it had made him very cautious about horses. "Ray Wilson is just up the street. He's watching us."

"We could get arrested," Danny said.

Lil looked at him. He had gone along with their pranks, but he had hardly said a word all evening. She wondered if Danny knew about Jay's dad being shipped overseas. She couldn't get it off her own mind. If it were her father, she knew she wouldn't be as brave as Jay was.

"It's getting late," Tootie said. "We'd better do Fancy Pantsy's. That's the big one."

"What are we going to do?" Lil said.

"Drive him crazy . . . what do you think? I'm going to paint terrible things on his door. He'll never get them out. It's nonwashable."

Suddenly Lil didn't want any part of this. She thought of what her father had said. Maybe Mr. Panzi acted odd because all his family had been killed in that pogrom thing. She tried to imagine having your whole family killed. Or even one. If Ernie were killed. "I'm going home," she said.

"Yellow—yellow—yellow," Tootie chanted. "Lil Adams is yellow."

Dinner at the Elks was over, and some people were coming out, laughing and talking. Up the street the big boys were whanging their cowbells and making a great racket. Lil saw Miss Smith come out, talking to another woman. She looked different in a brown silk dress and a hat with ribbons on it. Behind Miss Smith Lil saw Ruth Grant, the new girl from Rial Side, who had just moved to town with her parents and two older brothers. She was in the fifth grade, and already she and Lil had begun to be friends. Ruth was with her brothers, and she was dressed up as if she were going to a party. Lil shrank back out of Ruth's sight, feeling self-conscious in her costume.

"Ready for the attack," Charlie shouted. His cheeks were red with excitement.

There was a faint light inside Mr. Panzi's shop.

Jay grabbed her arm. "Come on, General, we might as well get this show over with. It's no-man's-land out there." But he didn't sound as if his heart was in it. When your own father was ordered overseas, it wasn't just a game anymore.

"It's only Halloween," Lil said.

Danny trotted beside her. He had lost Mary's belt, and he had to clutch his sheet to keep from tripping over it.

"What are we doing now?" he said, but no one answered him.

Charlie and Tootie reached the shoemaker's door at the same moment. Charlie began to pound on the door, yelling, "Kraut, Kraut, Sauerkraut! Hun-lover!" Tootie was using her brush and her blacking to write S-P-Y in huge letters that ran in uneven drips.

"Don't!" Lil said, but close as she was, no one could hear her.

The crowd in the street was pushing closer, yelling and banging on their dishpans and cowbells. Suddenly, a tall figure, with long gray hair blowing wildly, leaped to the step of the shoemaker's shop. It was Crazy Harry, his fiddle tucked under his arm. His usually smiling face was wrinkled with distress.

Somebody said, "It's Harry."

And someone else said, "He doesn't need a costume."

Harry held up his arm, and his high voice was shrill. "Please, children, stop," he called. He was almost drowned out by the laughter and shouts. "Please. Leave Mr. Panzi alone." He held up his fiddle. "Let me play for you." He tried, but the sounds were lost in the noise.

Lil was staring at him. Crazy Harry. Even his voice sounded different, more like other people's. She was half-aware that Danny was clinging to her arm.

"Don't let them hurt him," he said. "Lil, don't let them."

The door was flung open from the inside. It made Harry step backward. He lost his balance and would have fallen if so many had not crowded in around him.

"He's all right, Danny," Lil said.

"I want to go home," Danny said. But it was hard to move against the crowd.

Mr. Panzi was standing in the doorway. He reached for Charlie and missed, but he got hold of the front of Tootie's coat. Trying to break away, she threw the bottle of blacking, splashing it all over Mr. Panzi and anyone near him. Lil's white costume and Danny's sheet were splotched with black. Tootie pulled loose and ran.

Mr. Panzi was shouting and waving his arms. Tears streaked down his cheeks into his moustache. Lil and Danny were shoved closer by the pressure of people behind them. Lil couldn't see Jay anywhere.

Mr. Panzi's long arm shot out and grabbed Danny, shaking him, and he was shaking his other fist at the laughing crowd. More people were gathering, many out of curiosity, as more of the Elks party came out.

Lil saw John Kerrigan's red head as he dived through a knot of people and snatched a rock out of a boy's hand. Then he disappeared again, trying to make his way toward Mr. Panzi.

Lil grabbed Danny's free arm and tried to pull him away from Mr. Panzi's grip. Then she got her arm around his waist and tugged. Danny was being pulled both ways.

Some of the big boys began to chant, "Fancy Pantsy is a Hun. Light a fire and see him run!"

Lil's mask had been half knocked off, so it was hard to see. Then she was aware of somebody trying to loosen Mr. Panzi's grip. She shoved her mask back with a sweep of her arm, and saw that it was Miss Smith, her beribboned hat askew.

"Let him go, Mr. Panzi," she was shouting in his ear. "Let the child go."

He stared at her as if he didn't know who or what

she was. His chest was heaving, and his eyes were wild with fright.

"It's all right. Let the boy go."

The crowd had seen the word that Tootie had painted on Mr. Panzi's door, and they took up the chant: "*Spy! Spy! Spy!*"

Mr. Panzi let go of Danny and fell back against his door, his arm over his face.

"Get back!" Miss Smith was shouting. "Leave him alone. Where's Ray Wilson, for pity's sake!" She kept hold of Danny and Lil, steering them through the crowd to the street.

Suddenly Ray Wilson and Banty Moore were both there, scattering the crowd. Lil caught a glimpse of the ice lady, her face contorted, shouting, "Get him! He's a spy!" She looked strange without her ice tongs and her leather shoulder pad.

Miss Smith opened the passenger door of a white Pierce Arrow roadster. Janice Ward was sitting at the wheel. "Janice, take these children home." She pushed Danny and Lil inside and slammed the door. Danny had lost his jack-o'-lantern.

Janice drove down the street, looking back at the crowd. "What was that all about?"

Lil had her arm around Danny, who was shaking so much his teeth chattered. "They're after Mr. Panzi.

They're saying he's a spy."

"Oh, what nonsense," Janice said. "He's eccentric, but he's no more a spy than I am. Those stupid fools. Where does the little ghost live?"

"Asbury Grove."

"Oh, good. I've never been to the Grove. It's one of the ten thousand places my mother declared off-limits." She drove in silence for a few minutes. "Would you believe that I was never allowed to go out on Halloween the way you kids do?"

"You weren't?" Lil was thinking about Mr. Panzi. Would they hurt him? She wondered what had happened to Jay.

"Never. I was always at boarding school, and we'd have a nice party in the gym, bobbing for apples and eating little cakes with orange frosting and dreaming about boys and goblins and all the exciting things. What a life!"

Lil looked at her in surprise. She had always thought of Janice Ward leading the ideal life. "Do you know what a pogrom is?"

"A pogrom? I think it's where mobs go in and kill Jews. In places like Poland and Russia. Why?"

"I just wondered."

When they got to Danny's house, his father was sitting on the steps, smoking a pipe. He got up as the automobile stopped, and Danny ran up the steps and into his arms.

Janice backed the car out and turned around. "That's a handsome fellow, that kid's dad. What's his name?"

"Mr. Moe," Lil said. She felt dazed. When Janice let her out at her house, she barely remembered to thank her. Brushing off Mary's and her mother's questions, she went to bed and lay there shaking. She felt as if the war had spilled out of Europe and was right here in this town.

Chapter
THIRTEEN

◻|◻|◻|◻|◻|◻|◻|◻

"HAD TO PUT HIM in the drunk cage," Ray Wilson said. The soda fountain stool creaked under his massive weight. "They'd-a hurt him."

"Nobody blames you, Ray," Lil's father said.

Lil tried to get the last of her soda without making a slurping sound.

"What I wonder is, who called the Feds," Mr. Kelly said. He was wiping the marble counter with a damp cloth. "Don't see any need of that. We can take care of our own."

"Could have been any one of 'em," Ray said. "You get a crowd together, they go crazy. I heard about this fella out in the middle west, Pennsylvania or somewheres, they strung him up."

"You get the other side of the Hudson River," Mr. Blake, the hardware store owner, said, "they ain't civilized." He shook his head. "Poor old Panzi. Crazy as a coot but never hurt a fly."

"What will happen to him?" Lil asked. They all looked at her as if they had forgotten she was there.

"Oh, I guess they'll lock him up for a spell," Ray said.

"That's not fair!" she said.

"No, but he's better off that way than getting run out of town by a bunch of ruffians."

"They must have come from out of town," Mr. Blake said. "People ain't like that here."

"Ha!" Ray said, and made no further comment.

"What he needs is a lawyer," Lil's father said.

"I spoke to a couple of lawyers I know, but they wouldn't touch it," Ray said. " 'No, sir, not in this climate,' they said."

Lil's father sighed. "A while ago the president said, 'Once lead this people into war and they'll forget there ever was such a thing as tolerance.' "

Mr. Kelly shook his head and began to wash glasses.

Ray Wilson lifted his bulk off the stool and put fifteen cents on the counter. "Don't take any wooden nickels, fellas."

Mr. Blake followed him out.

"Well, Daughter," Lil's father said, "we'd better hit the trail for home, or we'll catch it for being late to supper. We'll see you, George."

"Ta-ta," Mr. Kelly said. He smiled at Lil and slid a Tootsie Roll across the counter. "Dessert."

"Thanks." She put it in the pocket of her coat.

Lil walked up the road with her father, scuffling through piles of leaves. The great elms were bare now, and their branches made black lacy patterns against the deep blue sky of dusk. The air smelled of bonfires. On the closed door of Mr. Panzi's shop someone had tried to wash out the word *spy*.

"It was my fault," she said.

"What was?"

"I gave that talk about spies. I said Mr. Panzi might be a German." She didn't mention the fact that she had suggested they paint his door.

He stopped and looked down at her. "Lil. It was not your fault. People have been spoiling to find a victim. In wartime all the worst in people comes out, as well as—sometimes—the best. They can't wait to tear somebody to pieces."

"You don't like war, do you?"

"I hate it. I was trained to save lives, not destroy them." He walked on, frowning. "I find it hard to believe that we can be as smart as we are, inventing things, discovering things, and still we settle disputes by slaughtering each other." He put his hand on her shoulder. "But don't think it was your fault. Just learn from it to watch your tongue. Sometimes the consequences of what we say and do are fearful indeed."

They crossed the street and went into their house, where Mary's dinner was smelling wonderful. Lil wondered what they fed people in jail.

The next evening right after supper Lil slipped out of the house and rode her bike to the field where the Home Guard drilled. It was a cold, drizzly night, and the leaves lay in sodden heaps on the ground. She rode into the field that had been a baseball field in happier times and sat down on the team bench.

On the field about two dozen men were being drilled by a man in a sergeant's uniform. Most of them had just come from work, and they looked tired and cold. In spite of the sergeant's efforts, the drilling was ragged. A few of them had real guns, but most of them used sticks.

Lil picked out Danny's father in the second row. She thought about Janice saying he was good-looking. She guessed he was. He looked younger than most of the fathers she knew.

She sat with her feet tucked under her, huddled against the chilly wind. The air smelled like snow. Jay said there was good sliding on the hill beyond Miles River, and when the river froze they could skate. The day before he had said to her, "I'm not going to play with Tootie anymore." She hadn't asked him why. She had just said, "Me either." During recess she had seen him playing with Danny, and she was glad.

The Home Guard drill ended, and the men drifted off toward home or toward the beer parlor or wherever they were going. Danny's father started across the field away from Lil. She got her bike and rode after him. At first he was talking to another man, but then they nodded to each other and separated.

"Mr. Moe . . ."

He stopped and looked at her. "Yes?"

She got nervous. He didn't look terribly friendly. The collar of his trench coat was turned up, and his hat was down over his eyes, so she could hardly see his face. "Uh . . . I'm Lil Adams. I'm a friend of Danny's. . . ."

His manner changed. He smiled at her. "The doctor's little girl."

"That's right."

"I want to thank you for being so nice to Danny. He enjoyed your party."

"Oh. Well, I'm glad he came." But she didn't want to talk about that. "Do you know Mr. Panzi?"

"By sight. I know what happened."

"He's in jail now, in Boston."

"I know." He stopped smiling. "It's an outrage."

"Well . . ." She wished she had thought this out more carefully. "He needs a lawyer. The ones around here are too yellow to help him. I wondered . . . I wondered if you knew any Socialist lawyers?" He looked surprised, and she plunged on. "I know lawyers cost money, but I'll put in my allowance. It's only two dollars a month, but maybe I could collect more from some of my friends. Maybe we could have a cookie sale or something."

He stared down at her for a moment. Then he said, "Let's talk." He walked over to one of the benches and sat down. "Why do you want to help Mr. Panzi?"

"Because he's being treated so mean."

"They say he's a spy."

"But I don't think he is. Now." She hesitated. "I was the one who said so first, though. He was so crabby, I thought he must be a spy."

He gave a tight little laugh. "I guess that makes as much sense as anybody else's reasons."

"His family were killed in a pogrom in Russia. I didn't know that till the other day. He probably has nightmares."

"I expect he does." When he pushed his hat onto the back of his head, he looked a little like Danny. "I could ask around."

She fished in her pocket and brought out sixty-five cents. "This is all I have left from this month, but you could give it to him for a start." She looked at his face to make sure he wasn't laughing at her. "I know lawyers cost a lot, but under the circumstances, since Socialists don't believe in war and all that, maybe . . ."

He interrupted her, putting his hand over hers. "You keep the money, Lillian. If I can find a Socialist lawyer to do this, I think he'll do it for free." He paused. "I think it might be a good thing if we didn't talk about this, though. People might not be too happy about it. Some people."

"Mum's the word."

He laughed and stood up. "We've got a deal." He shook her hand. "I'm glad I met you, Lillian."

"I'm glad I met you, too."

"I'll be in touch." He walked off into the deepening dusk.

"Well," she said aloud. "That is a nice man."

Chapter
FOURTEEN

0:0:0:0:0:0:0:0

LIL WAS WALKING home from school with her new friend, Ruth Grant, talking about Thanksgiving.

"We're going to have a twenty-pound turkey," Ruth said. "All my aunts and uncles and cousins are coming. My mother's been making mincemeat and stuff for weeks."

"Mine, too," Lil said, although it was really Mary who had been cooking. "I like squash pie better than mince pie, though." It wouldn't be the same without Ernie, but she was trying not to think about that. They still had not heard anything, and at night she had bad dreams about drowning and wrecked ships.

"Maybe the river will freeze hard enough so we can go skating. You and me and Jay." Ruth Grant was smitten with Jay. Lil thought it was very funny, because it embarrassed him so, but she knew he thought Ruth was pretty nice, too.

"And Danny," she said.

"Oh, sure, and Danny. I like Danny a lot. Not Charlie, though. He's too rough."

They paused after they crossed the railroad tracks.

"I heard about a kid that got his boot caught in these tracks, and he almost didn't get out before the train came," Lil said.

"I heard that, too, but I don't believe it." Ruth sneezed. "I'm catching a cold. What does your father do for a cold?"

"Blows his nose," Lil said, and nearly fell over laughing.

"Oh, you." Ruth was good-natured. "You'll be sorry when I get the grippe and have to stay in bed."

"I'll bring you Necco wafers. Bye." She waved and walked on toward her own house. She liked Ruth a lot. Ruth was a good sport.

She ran the last few yards. As soon as she changed her clothes, she was going to Jay's house to play with the telegraph set. Danny might be there, too. He was trying to learn the Morse code.

She leaped up the back steps and burst into the kitchen and then stood stock-still. Mary and Lil's mother were hugging each other and crying. "Ernie's dead!" Lil said.

They turned toward her, and she saw that they were smiling, tears and all.

"Oh, Lil, would you believe it!" Mary swooped down on her and almost smothered her in a hug. "It's a miracle, it is! I'm going to give me whole month's pay to the Virgin Mary."

Lil wiggled loose. "What are you talking about?"

"Oh, Lillian," her mother said, "we heard from Ernie! He's just a little bit wounded, but he's fine."

"And he's coming home!" Mary danced around the kitchen, flapping her apron.

"You have a letter of your own," her mother said. "It's on your bed."

Lil tripped over her own feet racing upstairs. There it was, lying on her bed, a letter addressed in Ernie's scrawl, with a strange stamp and blue letters on the back that said, "Passed by censor." She held it in her hands for a moment, almost afraid to open it. But they had said he was all right. Carefully she slit it open with her nail file.

"Dear Lil, How are you, kiddo? I am fine except for a busted shoulder and a few scratches. So excuse the writing. Not that it's ever much better (ha ha). I am alive and well, or pretty well anyhow, in jolly old [here the censor had blacked out a word] and I expect to come home soon. Practice up on 'Old Kit Bag.' And 'Anchors Aweigh.' I've still got a good right hand. Love, Ernie."

She read it over three more times. Jolly old blank was probably England. He wasn't likely to say jolly old anything else. She lay back on her bed. He was all right. He was alive. He was coming home. Whew! She leaped off the bed and did a somersault. After supper she would practice the piano. But now she had to tell Jay and Danny the news.

She changed her clothes with lightning speed and ran downstairs. "I'll be back," she cried, tossing her letter on the table so they could read it.

She zoomed into Jay's backyard on her bike, startling Archie and making him bark. She laughed then, remembering that Mrs. Collier had never figured out how Archie got a spinach leaf in his ruff. Mrs. Baxter never told.

The two boys were in the basement, working the telegraph. "Ernie's all right!" she shouted before she was even in the room.

Jay took off his earphones and looked at her. "That's great!"

"He's coming home!"

"That's great. Have you heard the news?"

"What news?"

Jay's face was pink with excitement. "Mama just told us. It came out in the paper, an extra. The English made a big tank attack, first one anybody ever tried."

"And they're winning!" Danny said.

"The war will probably end soon." Jay's eyes were bright. He took a deep breath. "Well, let's get back to the telegraph. Danny's learning real good."

Lil sat beside Danny at his table and waited for Jay's message. Maybe the war would end soon! The words ran through her head over and over like lines from a song.

HQ HQ HQ, came Jay's message. *Gen Collier to Gen Adams and Col Moe Prepare to back up British tanks. Stop. Expect heavy losses. Over.*

Danny and Lil studied the message that Lil had written down. "You go," she said to Danny.

"Can we pretend?" Danny said.

"Sure. It's all pretend anyway."

Danny put his hand on the key and leaned over to study the code book. Lil looked at Jay's bent head at the far end of the room. She knew he was thinking about his dad. They hadn't heard from him since he shipped out.

Slowly, stopping often to check the code book, Danny typed out his message. *Col Moe and Gen Adams to Gen*

Collier Now hear this Big Allied victory Stop War is over Stop Repeat War is over.

Lil pulled the key toward her and finished the message: *Peace Peace Peace Stop Over and Out.*

The three of them beamed at one another, as if something wonderful had happened. Lil flipped the set to receive, and they waited for Jay's message.

After a long pause Jay slowly tapped out his reply: *Collier to staff Hooray Stop.*